™

My name is Kara Zor-El. When I was a child, my planet, Krypton, was dying. I was sent to Earth to protect my cousin, but my pod got knocked off course, and by the time I got here, my cousin had already grown up and become Superman. I hid who I really was until one day when an accident forced me to reveal myself to the world.

To most people, I'm Kara Danvers, a reporter at CatCo Worldwide Media. But in secret, I work with my adoptive sister, Alex, for the Department of Extra-Normal Operations to protect my city from alien life and anyone else that means to cause it harm. I am . . .

RGIRL™

MASTER OF ILLUSION

BY JO WHITTEMORE

AMULET BOOKS
NEW YORK

TO ALL WHO ARE FORGOTTEN

Cataloging-in-Publication Data has been applied for and may be obtained from the Library of Congress.

ISBN 978-1-4197-3142-6

Cover Illustration by César Moreno
Book design by Chad W. Beckerman

Supergirl based on characters created by
Jerry Siegel and Joe Schuster.
By special arrangement with the Jerry Siegel family.

Amulet Books are available at special discounts when purchased in quantity for premiums and promotions as well as fundraising or educational use. Special editions can also be created to specification. For details, contact specialsales@abramsbooks.com or the address below.

ABRAMS The Art of Books
195 Broadway, New York, NY 10007
abramsbooks.com

1

WELCOME TO THE GALA, FRIENDS! Tickets, please? Thank you! Welcome to the gala, friends! Tickets, please? Thank you!"

"Belongings on the table, walk through the detector. Belongings on the table, walk through the detector."

The staff at National City's Fifth Annual Arts Gala operated with a rhythmic cadence, shuffling guests forward every few beats. One of those guests, Kara Danvers, shifted her weight from foot to foot, adjusting the bodice of her blue strapless gown as the procession neared the art museum's entrance.

While the people around her chatted about the *other* people around her, Kara peered past them, studying the scene inside the building and searching for story-worthy activity. Unlike most guests in line, Kara didn't care who came with whom or who had the nerve to show up so soon after his embezzlement scandal. As a journalist for *CatCo* magazine, she reported hard-hitting news, not gossip.

Unfortunately, the only activity in the museum seemed to be waitstaff meandering through a crowd of tuxedoed and gown-wearing guests, all of whom were either laughing or talking with heads bowed in close conversation.

Kara's glasses slid down her nose for the dozenth time, but she couldn't bring herself to pocket them. Along with the gown she was wearing, the glasses had come from her best friend Lena Luthor, and the color of the frames matched Kara's dress *and* eyes perfectly. It would've been even better if the frames were lead-lined to suppress Kara's X-ray vision, but that would've meant Lena knew Kara's biggest secret: that she was National City's resident hero, Supergirl.

Kara's clutch vibrated, and she fished out her cell phone.

Are you here yet? Lena's text message appeared on-screen. *You're missing the pot stickers.*

Kara groaned. "Aww, pot stickers!"

According to Lena, any time the art museum hosted a function, they served pot stickers made with Mangalitsa pork, a delicacy so delicious they were gone in minutes.

I'm stuck in line, Kara texted back. *Save me a coupledozen!*

she added as an afterthought, and returned to peering into the museum.

"Come *on*," she murmured at the line.

If Kara's sister, Alex, had been in this situation, she would've cut through the crowd, thrusting her credentials in the face of anyone who questioned her. But Alex was also the assistant director of a covert government organization, the Department of Extra-Normal Operations (DEO). She could intimidate someone just by raising an eyebrow.

On the opposite end of the spectrum, Kara's friend and CatCo CEO James Olsen would've charmed his way to the front of the line. But that came naturally to him. When Kara had tried to flirt her way into a club once, she'd asked the bouncer, "Don't I look like I belong here, handsome?"

His answer had been, "Maybe to do taxes . . . ma'am."

Somewhere between Alex and James was Winn Schott, one of Kara's best friends and the DEO's tech genius. *He* would've hacked into the gala's guest list and gotten a free VIP ticket. But VIP tickets were limited and brought in extra money for the museum's renovation project. Kara couldn't take funding from them.

Instead, she did what she always did best: adapt and accept . . . but not without a *little* pushback. Kara pressed closer to the people in front of her as if that might speed the line along, earning a dirty look from a man with a monocle.

"Do you mind?" Monocle Man asked in an affected tone.

"Sorry," Kara said with a smile and a wave. "I'm just really excited to see"—the man turned away—"your back as I'm talking to you," she finished.

Kara cleared her throat and adjusted her glasses, glancing around. She did a double take when she spotted another, much shorter, line at the far end of the museum. Squinting against the fading sunlight, Kara used her telescopic vision to read the sign above the archway: PRESS ENTRANCE.

"That's me!" she exclaimed. "I'm the press!"

Kara gathered her gown and hurried across the museum lawn. But the hurrying quickly turned to hobbling as her heels sank into the grass with each step.

"No one's watching, no one's watching," she chanted, even as she felt all eyes on her.

Kara fumbled with her clutch, pulling out her press pass as she reached the police officer checking IDs.

"Hell-o, Officer . . . Mercado," she said, reading his badge. She held up her own. "Kara Danvers with *CatCo* magazine." Kara flashed her best smile and hoped he wouldn't notice the trail of lawn destruction she'd left behind her.

Officer Mercado nodded at Kara's press pass. "Do you have your ticket?"

"Absolutely!" She reached into her clutch again. "I've got it right—"

Kara's fingers traveled over her phone, a pencil, and a steno pad, but found no ticket.

"Wait. It's here somewhere." She looked down at her clutch as she pawed through it. Her bag was big enough to hold the essentials but definitely not big enough to lose a colorful strip of paper. "Ohhh no."

Kara glanced back across the lawn. She'd left plenty of dirt clods and grass clippings behind, but no ticket.

She smiled up at Officer Mercado and chuckled nervously. "I don't seem to have it."

He chuckled, too, and stopped abruptly. "Then you can't go in."

Kara wiggled her phone. "But I have an e-mail where my boss mentioned giving it to me!" She held up a finger. "*And* I know that one corner of my ticket is bent."

Officer Mercado crossed his arms. "No ticket, no entry."

Kara pressed her hands together. "Please, sir. If you could just—"

"Kara Danvers! There you are!"

A dark-haired young man with a goatee and perfectly manicured eyebrows scurried down the museum steps, making a beeline for Kara. His purple jacquard suit drew glances from the crowd, but he appeared not to notice, his focus solely on her.

The only problem was that Kara had never seen this man in her life.

"Um, hi?" Kara greeted him with a small wave.

"What are you doing outside, silly thing?" The man hooked an arm through one of hers and looked her over. "Oh." He frowned at her grass-covered shoes. "You've been landscaping."

Kara pursed her lips and shifted her gown to cover her feet. "What are *you* doing out here . . . uh . . . buddy?"

"Lena and I have been waiting for you for ages," the man replied. "She sent me out to see what the holdup was."

"Lena." Kara relaxed at the mention of her best friend. "I'm sorry. I've been trying to get inside, but . . ." She let her sentence trail off and gestured to Officer Mercado.

"Ah. Say no more." The dark-haired man glanced at the police officer. "She's with me, hon." He tugged Kara toward the entrance, but Officer Mercado stepped in their path.

"And just who are *you*?" he asked.

"You're joking, right?" The dark-haired man drew himself to his full height and tucked his right hand into his jacket, looking a bit like a colorful Napoleon. "I know you recognize me."

There was a brief pause as Officer Mercado scrutinized the dark-haired man, and then his mouth fell open.

"Oh my . . . I'm so sorry." Officer Mercado removed his cap and stepped out of the dark-haired man's path. "Please. Go on in! Enjoy the gala!" Officer Mercado nodded to the ticket taker. "They're OK."

"OK?" The dark-haired man hooked his arm back through Kara's and scoffed. "Try great."

He winked conspiratorially at Kara, who grinned back, mystified. Whoever this guy was, he clearly had influence. Kara proceeded up the stairs beside the dark-haired man.

"Wow," she heard Officer Mercado whisper. "I just met Ed Sheeran!"

Kara wrinkled her forehead and glanced back.

Ed Sheeran?

Her right foot caught on the next step up, and Kara fell into someone on the landing.

To her chagrin, it was Monocle Man.

"Sorry! Sorry again," she said with a nervous chuckle, pointing at her feet. "Darn these new shoes!"

Monocle Man shot Kara his surliest look and blustered away.

Kara's dark-haired companion helped her stand. "That was the most elegant stumble since J.Law at the Oscars. Are you OK?"

Kara smoothed the front of her gown and pasted on a tight smile. "Yep. Just meeting my embarrassment quota for the day." She jabbed a thumb over one shoulder. "Did you know that police officer thought you were Ed Sheeran?"

"Seriously?" The dark-haired man frowned. "Poo! I hoped he knew who I was."

"*I* don't even know who you are," said Kara.

"Right! I'm so rude." The dark-haired man extended his hand. "Felix Foster."

"Kara Danvers," she replied with a firm handshake.

"Lena told me you work at CatCo. They own *Lunchtime with Laurie*, right?" Felix leaned closer. "Best daytime talk show ever. I never miss it."

"Oh! Well, I don't work on that show," Kara said, holding up her press pass. "I'm a journalist."

"For now." Felix eyed her pass. "Who knows? Maybe soon I'll see you on *Kibitzing with Kara*."

Kara laughed. "Anything's possible. So how do you know Lena?"

As if hearing the cue for her entrance, Lena Luthor sauntered over in a red off-the-shoulder gown.

"Felix and I just happen to share an interest in astrophysics," Lena explained, reaching out to clasp Kara's hands. "*You* look fabulous, by the way. I knew blue was your color."

Kara grinned and twirled once for Lena's inspection. "Thank you again for letting me borrow the dress. Oh, and thanks for the glasses!" She tapped them with an index finger. "They're perfect."

"I'm quite proud of myself for finding them," said Lena. "*And* for figuring out your prescription."

Kara's smile wavered only a little. Because of Earth's yellow sun, one of her superpowers was enhanced vision, which meant the glasses she typically wore had *zero* correction. They were just an effective disguise.

"Yeah, how . . . um . . . how *did* you figure that out?" Kara asked.

Lena stepped closer with a conspiratorial smile. "Remember our spa day? When you took off your glasses, I had my assistant run them to a lens store to make duplicates for the blue frames." Lena tapped her chin thoughtfully. "You know, your prescription was so weak, you probably don't even need glasses."

Kara chuckled. "Yeah, but I've worn them for so long, I'd be a totally different person without them." Before Lena could push the issue any further, Kara rubbed her hands together. "So . . . pot stickers?"

Lena pointed to a waiter standing amid a crowd of people. "I did a quick reconnaissance mission earlier, and that gentleman has a tray full of them."

The crowd parted, revealing an empty tray in the waiter's hand.

"*Had* a tray full of them," Lena corrected herself with a frown.

"Aw, man!" Kara approached the waiter. "Excuse me, where else can I get some of the pot stickers?"

"I'm sorry, but that was the last of them," the waiter said, tucking his tray under one arm.

"Perhaps there would've been more to go around if *someone* hadn't grabbed half the tray," a man grumbled, and shot a dirty look at a woman in furs whose plate was stacked high.

"I've got this," said Felix, approaching the woman as she downed one pot sticker after the other.

Kara turned to Lena with a smile. "Astrophysics, huh? Felix seems more like a PR guru."

"He's a theology professor, actually," Lena replied. "He came up and introduced himself after one of my innovation talks on dark matter last week. We talked for a bit about the dark matter detector L-Corp is working on."

"Dark matter?" Kara repeated. "Like, the stuff that makes up outer space? Why would a theology professor care about that?"

"God is in *all* the details, sweetie." Felix spoke from beside Kara. He held out a plate with three pot stickers. "And I believe these are yours."

Kara gasped and took the plate. "Felix! You are my hero twice tonight."

"If you ever feel compelled to write an article about

modern-day knights, I'm available for questions." He bowed slightly. "And now, if you ladies will excuse me, I see a handsome man across the room who needs rescuing from a dull conversation."

Kara and Lena exchanged an amused look as Felix sauntered away.

Kara set her plate and her clutch on a high-top table and was about to reach for the first pot sticker when a balding, scowling Latino man approached.

"Hey, Chief!" Kara greeted her boss, Snapper Carr. "Nice party, huh?"

"I feel like I'm trapped in a life-size game of Clue," he grumbled. Snapper pointed at Monocle Man, who was now talking to the woman in furs. "If you see either of them pick up a lead pipe, run."

Lena stifled a snicker and Kara smirked. "Not your usual crowd, boss?"

"Please," Snapper scoffed. "These posturing socialites are more on display than the art they're *pretending* to admire."

"At least it's for a good cause," Lena pointed out.

"The museum shouldn't have to throw a party to get support," Snapper countered. "These rich stiffs could just mail in donations." He eyed Kara's plate of food. "And I see you've got *your* priorities in order, Danvers. Pretentious food first, pretentious guests second?"

He grabbed one of Kara's pot stickers and popped it into his mouth. Kara squeaked in protest, and Snapper made a face.

"Ugh. Greasy." Nevertheless, he reached for a second.

"Boss!" Kara planted a hand in front of her two precious pot stickers. "I'm sure you didn't walk over here just to discuss board games and insult party guests."

Snapper withdrew his hand and wiped his fingers on his shirtfront. "You're right. I wanted to make sure you knew that the press pass you're wearing is for more than spreading caviar on crackers."

Kara smirked. "I'm aware. I'm here to cover the gala, and when anything interesting happens, I'll be sure to jot it down." She reached into her clutch and pulled out her steno pad.

Snapper stared at Kara, unblinking. "Oh, thank God," he said in a monotone voice. "You'll be able to catch the same sound bite as twenty other reporters." He banged a fist on the high table, making the pot stickers, Kara, and Lena jump. "Wake up, Danvers! Covering this gala doesn't win the Wheeler-Nicholson Award. Meeting people with interesting stories does. *That's* the real reason you're here."

"The Wheeler-Nicholson Award?" Lena repeated. "What's that?"

"It's this area media award given to one new journalist

every year," Kara explained. She nodded in Snapper's direction. "*Someone* submitted my articles on the alien fight club and the supercitizens to the awards committee, and as of yesterday, I'm . . . kind of a finalist." She shrugged modestly even as a broad grin spread across her face.

"Kara, that's wonderful!" exclaimed Lena.

One of the bonuses of being a journalist and superhero was access to inside information. When the villain Roulette had run an alien fight club to profit off National City's elite gamblers, Supergirl had been in the ring to defeat one of the biggest contenders and shut it down. When National City's citizens had developed temporary superpowers from an ancient Atlantean metal, Supergirl had stopped the Atlantean metal from being further abused and distributed.

The only downside of sharing this information with the public was that Snapper frowned on Kara constantly using Supergirl as a source, so Kara had to work extra hard cultivating other sources that could corroborate her information. And, based on her Wheeler-Nicholson nod, it looked like her hard work was starting to pay off.

"It's wonderful *if* she can clinch the award with a show-stopping article, which she can't get standing around with you," Snapper told Lena. "As much as I loathe and disparage these people, they're high-powered influencers with stories that earn prime placement on the magazine rack."

He scowled at Kara and pointed to the other gala guests. "Mingle and get their stories."

Kara snorted. "You act like it's as easy as walking up to someone and saying 'Hi.' I have to check things out first, sniff out the story."

Snapper sighed, cracked his neck, and cleared his throat. Then he pasted on a huge grin and approached Monocle Man, tapping him on the shoulder. "*Hi*. Sorry to bother you, but I just wanted to say how much I love that time-piece of yours!" Snapper gushed, pointing at Monocle Man's pocket watch. "My abuelo, God rest his soul, had one just like it." Snapper placed a hand to his heart.

As Kara watched Snapper's act, her mouth fell open. He was so friendly, so warm, so . . . normal.

It was kind of freaking her out.

"Why, thank you for noticing!" said Monocle Man. "You know, there's quite an interesting story about how I came to own it."

"An interesting *story*, you say?" Snapper repeated with a sideways glance at Kara. "Well, I'd love to hear it." He handed Monocle Man a business card. "Snapper Carr, *CatCo* magazine. Give me a call sometime."

Snapper snapped his fingers and pointed at Monocle Man before walking back to Kara and Lena, his face returning to its usual joyless state.

Kara fiddled with her glasses. "OK . . . well . . . you said a lot more than 'Hi,'" she pointed out.

"Mingle and get those stories, Danvers," Snapper repeated.

"For your information, I *have* been working on a story." Kara studied the crowd. "With . . ."

"You're going to make up a name? This ought to be good," Snapper muttered. "Let me guess . . . Bob Tablecloth? Sally Carving Station?"

Kara's eyes fell on a tall Hispanic woman in a daring gold dress who stood in a far corner. Gold bracelets clinked on her wrists as she told an animated story to National City's mayor and district attorney.

Kara had met this woman once before. *And*, she thought smugly, the woman was a princess. Ultimate interview material.

"Her!" Kara pointed to the Hispanic woman and struggled to recall her name. "Princess T . . . Tuhhh—" She tapped her forehead.

"Princess Tlaca," Lena supplied. "We met her at the National City Symphony a few weeks ago."

Snapper scrutinized the princess. "Oh, right. She did an episode of *Lunchtime with Laurie*."

"You watch that show?" Kara couldn't keep the surprise out of her voice.

Lunchtime with Laurie was known for being light and funny. Snapper . . . not so much.

"It came up in CatCo's weekly management meeting," Snapper replied. "Apparently, the studio had trouble balancing the sound because Princess Tlaca was wearing those ridiculous clunky bracelets."

"Hey, there's nothing wrong with accessorizing." Kara's hands rested on her hips. "And to get back to *my* point, when I met her at the symphony, I asked for an interview," she informed Snapper.

He stared at Kara. "And?"

Kara jumped into action. "And . . . I'm going to follow up on it right now."

She ventured toward the princess, paused, and scrambled back to grab her last two pot stickers, shoving them both into her mouth.

"Mmmoh, my gosh!" she exclaimed around a mouthful of pork.

"Right?" said Lena. She placed a hand on Kara's arm and steered her away from Snapper. "Listen, Snapper's approach makes sense, but you do have other options to win this award. You can go ultramodern."

"Ultramodern?" Kara repeated, covering her still-stuffed mouth with one hand.

Lena nodded. "Technology holds a lot of appeal these

days. Surely, you've seen all the buzz about private space-flight companies? I can set you up with one of their business directors like *that*." She snapped her fingers.

Kara chewed and nodded, using it as an excuse not to answer. Since Lena was the busy CEO of a billion-dollar tech company, Kara appreciated that she was willing to go out of her way to help find a story, but Kara knew in her heart that writing about tech wasn't the best option for her. After all, the stories that had made Kara a finalist had been about fight clubs and ancient Atlantean metal . . . very low-tech. And Kara liked writing stories that benefited everyone around her, either exposing and eliminating threats to the city or inspiring people to follow their better angels, just like her alter ego, Supergirl, did.

She knew that Snapper also meant well, despite his gruff demeanor, but his drive to sell magazines wasn't *her* drive. Kara had never had to rub elbows with influencers to get stories before. She didn't see this as the time to start.

But Snapper *was* watching Kara at the moment. And he controlled her paycheck.

Kara swallowed and smiled at Lena. "Thanks for the offer. I'll give it some thought," she promised.

She swiped at her face with a napkin, threw back her shoulders, and marched toward Princess Tlaca, waiting for a break in the princess's conversation to close the gap.

"Princess Tlaca? I don't know if you remember me, but I'm Kara Danvers."

Thinking of Snapper's earlier example, Kara tucked her clutch under one arm and wrapped both hands around Princess Tlaca's right one, going for a warm and hearty handshake. The other woman jerked her hand back with a scowl, bangles rattling.

"What exactly did you want, Miss Danvers?" the princess asked in a deep, husky voice.

Kara blinked up at Tlaca, confused by the brusque response. "I . . . I . . . was just hoping to interview you." She withdrew her hands, folding and unfolding them across her stomach. "For *CatCo* magazine."

A woman in a satiny silver jumpsuit stepped forward and whispered something in the princess's ear. Princess Tlaca's eyes widened and her expression softened.

"*CatCo*, yes, of course! I apologize," said the princess. "I would be happy to talk as long as we can discuss my indigenous peoples' foundation, The Forgotten. Raising money for them is the main reason I am here."

A princess with a foundation to help indigenous peoples? Kara thought. *The article practically writes itself!*

"Absolutely," she told Princess Tlaca.

"Excellent. I have meetings all day tomorrow, but I will fit you in." Princess Tlaca turned to her companion. "Chimalli?"

The woman in the silver jumpsuit pulled a cell phone from her pocket and studied the screen. "Will ten o'clock in the morning work?"

"That would be perfect," Kara said, getting out her own phone. "Thank you so much."

"It is my pleasure," said Princess Tlaca as Chimalli handed Kara a business card with the appointment scribbled on the back.

"My readers will love this. I mean, it's not every day we get a princess *here!*" Kara said, sweeping her arms out just as a waiter bustled past with a tray of champagne flutes.

The waiter did his best to steady the glassware, but several still tipped and crashed to the floor, spraying Princess Tlaca with champagne.

"Oh my gosh!" Kara's hands flew to her mouth. "I am *so* sorry. Let me get—" She glanced around for something to blot the stains spreading over the princess's dress.

Princess Tlaca waved a dismissive hand. "Please. There is no need to fuss. I can tidy up in the restroom." She and Chimalli stepped away from their corner, bumping into Felix as he walked past with another gentleman.

Felix watched the princess and her assistant bustle away. "No, no. *I'm* sorry," he grumbled.

"It's my fault they're so distracted." Kara bit her lip. "I . . . happened."

Felix glanced at the sticky pools of sparkling liquid. "You know, most people just send champagne back if they don't like it."

Kara gave a pained laugh. "What can I say? I like to leave an impression."

"Can we help?" the gentleman with Felix asked.

Kara shook her head and pushed her glasses up the bridge of her nose. "Thanks, but this is my mess to clean up. Literally."

At least she'd gotten an appointment with the princess. *If* the woman still wanted to keep it.

"If you need us, we'll be enjoying the gardens," Felix said, arm in arm with his companion.

Kara gave a little wave. "Stop and smell the roses for me." She dropped to her knees beside the waiter and began collecting shards of glass as people strolled and swished by.

"I'm so sorry," Kara told the waiter, braving a glance in Snapper's direction. Luckily, her boss was deeply engrossed in conversation with someone and didn't appear to have seen her spectacular self-sabotage.

The waiter smiled at Kara. "Don't worry about it. These aren't the first drinks to be spilled tonight, and they won't be the last." He shooed her away. "Go enjoy the gala. I don't want you to get cut."

"Oh, I can't . . ." Kara stopped herself. She'd been about to let slip that she *couldn't* be cut, since her skin was impervious to harm, save from kryptonite and magic. "I can't let you do this alone," she finished.

"Please, I insist," the waiter said. "You're missing all the fun."

Kara straightened and stared at Princess Tlaca's business card still clutched in her hand. Maybe if she sent apology flowers to the princess's hotel, it would make for a smoother interview. She could even visit the museum garden right now to see which blooms would be best.

Pleased with that idea, Kara managed three steps toward the garden's French doors before a screaming, purple-clad figure flew head over heels past the exit. Other partygoers gasped and rushed forward, Kara leading the pack.

"Felix!" she shouted, running in the direction she'd seen him fly.

Luckily, he'd landed in a hydrangea bush, so he was fairly unharmed . . . physically, at least. The expression on Felix's face was one of sheer terror.

"She's . . . she's a madwoman!" he sputtered, pointing behind Kara.

"She's trying to kill us!" Felix's companion cried from behind a nearby trellis.

"Who?" Kara glanced over her shoulder. The party guests had begun to crowd the doorway, but they all looked just as startled as she did.

Kara turned back to Felix, who was still pointing. This time, however, she noticed his finger was tilted up. Slowly, Kara turned and looked skyward.

There, floating above the garden, was Princess Tlaca. And in one hand, she held a fireball.

2

WHOA!" KARA EXCLAIMED. "NO!"

Princess Tlaca hurled the fireball at Felix, who struggled to free himself from the hydrangea. Kara lunged forward and grabbed his arm, yanking Felix from the bushes just as they ignited in a fiery explosion.

"O-K." Felix let out a shaky breath. "I officially hate gardens."

"Grab your friend and hide behind that arch." Kara pointed toward a stone fixture. "I'll get help."

Felix gazed up at Princess Tlaca, then down at his purple suit. "Suddenly, camouflage tuxedos make *so* much sense."

"Go!" Kara pushed him before sprinting around the corner of the museum, while tugging off her glasses. Quick as a flash, she zipped out of her blue evening gown and into her blue-and-red Supergirl ensemble.

An alarmed shout from the garden sent Supergirl skyward, directly into the path of Princess Tlaca's second fireball. Supergirl twisted in midair so the flames struck her cape, but fiery shrapnel bounced off the fabric and popped against her neck.

"Ah!" Supergirl swatted at the embers, rubbing her singed skin.

Skin that was impervious to earthly harm.

Which meant Princess Tlaca was using magic.

Supergirl spun to face her, unleashing a torrent of freezing breath.

The princess raised her arms to shield herself, and the third fireball in her palm was instantly extinguished.

"Stand down!" Supergirl commanded. "Stand down, or I'll force you down."

"Ha!" Felix peeked out from behind the arch. "Didn't expect *that*, did you, Princess Pyro?"

"Get back into hiding!" Supergirl shouted. Felix quickly disappeared.

"Supergirl." Princess Tlaca narrowed her eyes and lowered her arms. "You disappoint me. I thought we could be allies."

Supergirl scoffed. "You think I'd ally myself with someone who attacks innocent people?"

"He is not innocent!" Princess Tlaca jabbed a finger at Felix's hiding place. "He stole something that belongs to me! He bumped into me in the museum, and now it is gone."

Supergirl kept her expression neutral, but Princess Tlaca's words sparked recognition. She was referring to the moment after the champagne disaster.

"Stay here." Supergirl swooped down, landing next to Felix's hiding place. "Is that true?" she asked him. "Did you steal from that woman?"

Felix shook his head, wide-eyed. "I swear, I don't know what she's talking about."

"Liar!" Despite Supergirl's command, Princess Tlaca touched down, too, and stormed toward Felix. Supergirl barred her path with one arm.

"Easy." Supergirl fixed Princess Tlaca with a stern expression. "What did he take?"

Princess Tlaca lifted her chin and sniffed. "My bracelet."

Supergirl's eyes widened. "You want to kill this man over a piece of jewelry?"

Princess Tlaca set her lips in a thin line. "It is very special *jewelry*." She said the last word in a contemptuous tone, and Supergirl recalled the princess jerking her hand back when Supergirl's alter ego, Kara, had tried to shake it. Now Supergirl understood why.

But she still didn't approve.

Supergirl looked at Felix. "Do you have this woman's bracelet?"

Again, Felix shook his head and began emptying his pockets. "See? Breath mints, a pocket watch, my house keys . . ." He held them all out. "And my wallet is in my back pocket, but that's all."

Supergirl crossed her arms and stared at Felix, using her X-ray vision to see if he was telling the truth. Sure enough, with the exception of his clothes, there was nothing else on Felix's person.

"He doesn't have the bracelet," Supergirl informed Princess Tlaca. "You've got the wrong guy."

"Then his companion has it!" Princess Tlaca ducked past Supergirl, but the gentleman hiding with Felix emerged, hands above his head.

"M-m-my name is Tim Lambert. I'm an accountant at Pierce-Wodehouse," he recited nervously, "and my mother taught me never to take what isn't mine."

Supergirl couldn't help smiling. "Thank you, Tim." She turned back to Princess Tlaca. "Maybe you dropped the bracelet. Or maybe someone *else* took it. Either way, you can't keep attacking these people without proof."

"That's right." Felix tucked his hand into his jacket, striking his earlier regal pose. "Due process of law. I'm entitled."

"*No.*" Princess Tlaca stepped closer to Supergirl, who

clenched both fists at her sides, ready for a fight. "The bracelet was secured with magic, so only *magic* could remove it." She glanced across the garden at the crowd that was still gathered in the doorway. Several people were now holding cameras and phones in the air to capture everything. In a hushed voice, Princess Tlaca added, "Jason Blood tasked me with protecting it. And he said I could count on you."

Supergirl unclenched her fists. "Jason?" she repeated.

Not long ago, a Roman patrician named Gaius Marcus had cursed National City, turning it into a facsimile of Ancient Rome. It was only with Jason Blood's help that Supergirl and the DEO team had been able to reverse the curse. Reversing the curse had also reversed time, and up until now, Supergirl had thought she was the only one who remembered what happened. Apparently, Jason remembered, too.

Princess Tlaca nodded. "He said you could help me if ever I was in trouble. And now, I am in trouble. This whole *world* could be in trouble."

Supergirl shook her head and chuckled humorlessly. "You *really* should've led with that. OK, let's—" She stepped away from Tlaca to face Felix, but he was no longer there. "Where'd your friend go?" she asked Tim.

Tim glanced around with a start. "I don't . . . I didn't see him leave."

"Magic." Princess Tlaca swore under her breath. "This is why you should have let me deal with him!"

Supergirl opened her mouth, then closed it again. She did this a few more times before she finally found the words. "Sit tight," she said, leaping into the air. She hovered above the museum and scanned the area for the impossible-to-miss purple suit, but Felix was nowhere to be seen. She used her X-ray vision to search the museum for Felix and the bracelet.

Nothing.

"Any luck?" Princess Tlaca asked as Supergirl touched down.

She shook her head. "And in my experience, innocent people don't flee a crime scene. Did anyone see where the man in the purple suit went?" she asked, approaching the crowd.

They glanced at one another but shook their heads.

Supergirl ushered them through the doors. "All right then. Back inside, please. Show's over."

People in the crowd groaned but slowly shuffled into the museum.

"Supergirl!" A woman from one of CatCo's rival news stations pushed her way against the crowd, tape recorder held aloft. "What's going on here? Who *is* the man in purple?"

Supergirl sucked air through her teeth. Even though her

alter ego was a member of the press, she'd forgotten they were in attendance.

Another reporter held up his cell phone as he stepped closer. "Is the man in purple guilty or innocent?"

"Is it true he's related to Ed Sheeran?" another reporter asked.

Supergirl faced them all with hands on hips. "I'm honestly not sure *who* he is anymore." She eyed each reporter as if they were the most important person in the world. "But if you see him, you'll report it to Maggie Sawyer at the National City Police Department, won't you? You won't broadcast it and scare him away?"

In addition to being the DEO's contact at NCPD, Maggie was also Alex's girlfriend and one of the few people outside the DEO who knew Supergirl's secret identity. She knew she could trust Maggie to be discreet. She hoped the same could be said for these reporters.

The reporters jotted down notes and slowly nodded their agreement. Supergirl smiled.

"I knew I could count on all of you, the true heroes of National City."

The reporters grinned at her and one another, puffing out their chests and strutting back into the museum. Supergirl rubbed her temples and trudged over to Princess Tlaca, who was talking with Tim.

"I'm sorry." Tim's arms were raised in a shrug. He seemed less nervous now that the princess was no longer throwing fireballs. "I just met him. But Felix seemed like a nice enough guy."

"Wait a minute." Princess Tlaca's eyebrows lifted. "His name is Felix?"

Tim nodded. "Felix Foster."

Princess Tlaca's expression twisted into a mixture of realization and horror.

"Do you know him?" Supergirl asked.

The princess sighed and wrung her hands together. "If he is who I think he is, his true name is Felix Faust, and we are all in grave danger."

Tim paled. "Danger?"

"You said something like that earlier." Supergirl pulled Princess Tlaca away from Tim so they could speak privately. "Explain."

Eyes darting around for eavesdroppers, the princess spoke in low, urgent tones. "That bracelet contained a charm, the Jar of Calythos, one of three artifacts used to unleash the Demons Three . . . ."

Supergirl jerked back. "DE—" At a warning look from Princess Tlaca, Supergirl lowered her voice. "Demons?"

It wasn't that Supergirl had never faced one. On the contrary, Jason Blood's alter ego was a demon named Etrigan.

But Etrigan, while a little unpredictable, had been on the side of good. Something told Supergirl these other demons wouldn't be.

Princess Tlaca nodded. "The Demons Three possess very powerful magic—a hundred times more powerful than mine—that transfers to whoever releases them. According to Jason, the men who have released the demons in the past have used this power for unspeakable horrors."

"Such as?" Supergirl asked, though she wasn't sure she wanted to know.

"Genocide. Regicide. Once, Faust used the demons to plant fear in the hearts of the Aztec people—my ancestors—turning them to war and crumbling their empire."

"The Aztecs?" Supergirl racked her brain for the world history she—or rather, *Kara Danvers*—had learned in school. "That was over five hundred years ago."

Princess Tlaca nodded solemnly. "Yes, it was long ago. But the fact remains, Faust is responsible for bringing great suffering to my people."

Supergirl glanced at the spot where she'd last seen Felix. Granted, she'd known him a short time, but she never expected him to be capable of such evil.

"Why would he do this?" she asked.

"The Flame of Life," Tlaca replied. "It came about in the fifth millennium BCE, and it allowed its keeper to prosper, his civilization to flourish. Faust tried to steal the flame with the help of the demons, but he was banished to another dimension while the demons were sealed inside three artifacts: the Bell of Ulthool, the Wheel of Nyorlath, and the Jar of Calythos. Ever since Faust's return from that dimension, he has sought the civilization that holds the flame. If he thinks a people might possess it, he destroys them. Or rather . . . he forces them to destroy one another."

"Sweet Rao." Supergirl whispered the Krypton deity's name and brought her hands to her temples. "You mentioned some other artifacts besides the Jar of Calythos?"

"Jason received word that the Wheel of Nyorlath had been taken a month ago," the princess continued. "He went in search of the Bell of Ulthool and wanted me to guard the Jar of Calythos, which had been left in his care. That was why he and I met the last time I was here."

"So he could give you the jar," Supergirl guessed.

"He also gave me a list of people who might be after the artifacts, but"—the princess shook her head—"I did not expect one to be a guest at this gala. If Faust stole the Wheel of Nyorlath and now has the Jar of Calythos, all he needs is the Bell of Ulthool."

"At which point he can release the demons and use their power for who knows what," Supergirl finished, setting her lips in a tight line. "And I let him get away."

She felt like kicking herself.

"What do we do now?" Princess Tlaca asked. "Faust has already decimated my ancestors. I refuse to let his ruthless terror continue or to let him destroy another civilization. Something tells me you feel the same."

"I do." Supergirl's eyes traveled from Tim to the garden doors, where the reporters had stood only moments before. "All right. First, we say nothing about what's really missing. The last thing we need is to incite a panic."

Princess Tlaca nodded. "Agreed."

"Second, we visit some friends of mine who can help." Supergirl walked back to where Tim was waiting and held a hand out. "Can I borrow your tie?"

Tim looked down at his suit. "My tie? Sure."

He loosened it and passed it to Supergirl, who handed it to Princess Tlaca. At the questioning look in the princess's eyes, Supergirl said, "I need you to put this on as a blindfold. We're going to a secret government installation. You can't know its location."

"Of course not," said Princess Tlaca. "Because that would be the *worst* thing to happen right now." Still, she wrapped the tie around her head and secured it like a blindfold.

"Tell the museum chairs we're sorry for the mess," Supergirl told Tim. "And tell Princess Tlaca's assistant that she's safe with me."

"Uh . . . sure," he said with a nod.

Supergirl wrapped one arm around Princess Tlaca to guide her and lifted with her into the air. "Hang on tight and follow me."

Moments later, the duo landed on the DEO balcony, earning surprised looks from several agents working the floor. After removing the princess's blindfold, Supergirl led her to the control room, where a tall, dark-haired man sat reading *Romeo and Juliet*. Despite the current predicament, Supergirl smiled at her boyfriend, Mon-El of Daxam.

"Hey, Romeo?" Supergirl touched his shoulder.

Mon-El lowered the book and swiveled toward her. "Hey, ba . . . by corn is delicious," he said, amending his sweet talk when he saw the stranger with her. Mon-El waved at Princess Tlaca. "Hello. I like baby corn."

Princess Tlaca blinked at him. "All right."

Supergirl suppressed a smile. "Mon-El, this is Princess Tlaca." She gestured to the woman, who made a tutting sound.

"Please. Just call me Tlaca."

Mon-El rose from his chair. "Tlaca, nice to meet you." He extended a hand to the princess, who shook it. "What brings you here?"

"Trouble," said Tlaca.

"Ahhh, trouble." Mon-El rubbed his palms together.

"Something we excel at getting into *and* out of. Which is it this time?"

"*I* got us into trouble," Supergirl said, "and *we* need to get us out of it. Where are Director Henshaw and Alex?"

Mon-El gestured down the control room steps. "They're with the new recruits in the training simulator. What are we up against?"

"Not what . . . who." Supergirl started down the steps with Tlaca on one side and Mon-El on the other. "A man named Felix Faust. He stole an artifact."

"Not a harmless artifact, I'm guessing." Mon-El pointed to Supergirl's forehead. "Or you wouldn't have the crinkle."

Supergirl reached up and smoothed the space between her eyebrows. "Faust stole something that, combined with two other objects, could unleash a trio of demons."

"What?" Mon-El's laughter echoed down the corridor. "There's no such thing as demons."

"Trust me, there are," said Supergirl. "And they have magic, which we're both vulnerable to." She gestured to herself and him.

Mon-El's home world of Daxam was a sister planet to Supergirl's home world of Krypton, giving him similar powers to hers along with the shared weakness against magic.

"We are?" Mon-El frowned as Supergirl opened the door to the training simulator. "How do you know?"

"Tlaca threw a fireball at me earlier," she said, pointing to a burn on her neck. "And it hurt."

The trio entered the training simulator, which was dark save for a track of lights bordering the room and leading up to an observation deck. From there, Supergirl's auburn-haired sister, Alex, barked orders to the recruits.

"Hurley, watch your six! Wilson, a low crawl should be just that! Get your butt down!"

Beside her stood a tall, middle-aged black man who was actually a tall, centuries-old Green Martian in disguise. To everyone outside the DEO, he went by the name Hank Henshaw. To everyone inside, he was known as J'onn J'onzz.

"Remember, only fools rush in!" J'onn called. "Take your time and secure the perimeter. Supergirl, I don't like strangers in my building," he said without missing a beat or glancing in her direction.

Supergirl floated up to the observation deck. "I know, but I had to bring her." She gestured down at Tlaca. "She was guarding something important that was stolen, and if we don't catch the thief, he'll unleash demons and use their power for evil."

"What . . . demons?" Alex glanced over. "Are you serious?"

"Yes." Supergirl fixed her sister with a stare. "And if you're secretly a demon slayer, now would be a great time to say so."

J'onn smirked. "We face evil every day, Supergirl. You'll have to be more—"

"Civilization-ending evil," she amended. "This guy was behind the fall of the Aztec Empire and who knows what else."

Alex and J'onn shared a look. The DEO director gave a slight nod, and Alex pressed a button on a control panel in front of her. Instantly, light from overhead filled the room, and the recruits turned to the observation deck.

"All right, recruits, take a break!" Alex called to them. "When we resume, I want to see better than this. Espinoza, work on your signals. Parker, work on your speed. Hurley, lose the gum."

Two female recruits nodded, and one of the male recruits spit something into his hand.

Supergirl lowered herself to the ground while Alex and J'onn descended the ladder. After introductions were exchanged with Tlaca, the DEO agents and the princess returned to the control room, while Supergirl explained what she'd witnessed in the museum garden.

"And how are *you* wrapped up in all of this?" Alex asked Tlaca.

"There is a man, a demonologist named Jason Blood," Tlaca explained. "He came to my village in Mexico a few years ago, looking for a *Homo magi*, a human born into magic. That is what I am."

"Magic?" J'onn repeated, leaning against the control room conference table. "As in . . ."

"As in magic," Tlaca said simply. "It is in my family's bloodline. We are descendants of a powerful Aztec priest who was granted the gifts of Xiuhtecuhtli, the god of fire."

"There's something you don't hear every day," Alex commented. "So, your specialty is . . ."

"Pyrokinesis," said Tlaca. "I can create and control fire, even using the residual heat of it to fly. Jason helped me hone my gift in exchange for future assistance." She clasped her hands together. "And last month he came to me with a problem."

"Someone had stolen the Wheel of Nyorlath," Supergirl interjected, and Tlaca nodded.

"This wheel . . . how big is it?" Mon-El asked, holding his hands apart. "Are we talking hamster, car, or 'I'd like to buy a vowel'?"

"It can fit in the palm of your hand," Tlaca said, cupping hers. "But its power is immeasurable. When Jason learned the Wheel of Nyorlath was stolen, he had a list of suspects but no discernible lead," Tlaca continued. "He brought the Jar of Calythos to me for protection while he went searching for the last item: the Bell of Ulthool."

"And then Faust stole the jar from you," J'onn finished. "May I see this list?"

Tlaca reached into the folds of her dress. "I still do not know how Faust tracked the artifact to me." As she pulled a notebook from her pocket, her bracelets clanked loudly against one another.

Bracelets, Supergirl recalled, that Snapper had said drowned out Tlaca's interview on *Lunchtime with Laurie*. Bracelets that had held charms, one of which had been the Jar of Calythos.

"Did Jason give you the jar before you were on *Lunchtime with Laurie*?" Supergirl asked.

Tlaca blinked at her, nonplussed. "Why, yes. How did you know I was on the show?"

"Oh, my boss—" Supergirl cut herself off when she realized she was responding as Kara Danvers. "My boss . . ."

Her eyes flitted to her sister, who watched her with raised eyebrows.

One of the downsides of Supergirl's secret identity was not always being able to share what that secret identity knew. Which also meant Supergirl couldn't share that Faust watched *Lunchtime with Laurie* religiously. He'd no doubt spotted the jar on Tlaca's bracelet when she was on TV.

"*I* watch the show every day," J'onn chimed in. "I'm her boss." He pointed at Supergirl. "And I saw *you* on it." He pointed at Tlaca.

To Supergirl's relief, Tlaca's expression relaxed.

"I see." Tlaca passed J'onn the notebook and turned to Supergirl. "You think that show is how Faust knew I had the Jar of Calythos?"

Supergirl attempted a casual shrug. "Maybe," she said. *Definitely*, she thought.

J'onn flipped through the notebook, shaking his head. "Felix Faust aka Felix Foster aka Felix Faustenhammer aka Felix Fausto."

"A rose by any other name would smell as sweet," Mon-El intoned.

The others looked at him curiously.

"What?" he asked. "It's *Romeo and Juliet*."

"Except in this case, we're definitely not dealing with a rose," said Supergirl. "More like a thorn."

"So, we have to get both the Wheel of Nyorlath *and* the Jar of Calythos back from Faust in case he reaches the Bell of Ulthool before Jason," said Alex. "Agent Vasquez?" She turned to a Latina woman with short-cropped dark hair who was seated nearby. "Do a search in all criminal databases for Felix Faust aka Foster aka—"

Agent Vasquez didn't move. "Already done, ma'am. No records of him under the names Director Henshaw mentioned."

Supergirl chewed her lip. "Faust can't have gotten far.

Can we get a museum camera capture of his face sent to NCPD and security personnel at the airport and train stations?"

"We can," said Alex, "but I don't think he'll flee the city just yet. If he's as crafty as he sounds, he knows we'll take that step, so he'll lie low wherever he is."

"How about using traffic cameras to catch him?" suggested Mon-El.

"I'm not certain that'll work with Faust." J'onn held up the notebook. "Apparently, he's a *Homo magi* like Tlaca, but unlike her, his skill isn't pyrokinesis; it's illusion conjuring."

"What?" Tlaca reached for her notebook. "Where do you see that?"

J'onn pointed to a page. "This note here: *Entrances the eye; procidat deceptionem.* Those last two words are Latin for 'illusion.'"

"Very impressive," Alex commented, bumping his shoulder.

Supergirl had to agree . . . and envy J'onn a little. When the Atlantean metal, orichalcum, had given National City's citizens superpowers, it had also given Supergirl the power to understand anyone, which came in handy when National City had been reverted to Ancient Rome. Unfortunately, translating all that Latin had used most of the orichalcum in her system, and Supergirl had lost her new power.

"Okay, so Faust's an illusion conjurer," Mon-El said, bringing Supergirl back to the present. "How does that affect traffic cameras?"

"It doesn't affect the cameras," Supergirl said with a deep sigh. "It affects Faust. If he's good with illusions, he can probably make himself look like anyone." She shrugged. "Heck, he might not even own a purple suit or have a goatee. He could be running around in pajamas and a . . . a shaved head. Or he could even look like Ed Sheeran," she added, remembering what the police officer at the gala had seen.

Alex paced in front of the conference table. "In other words, we're looking for a guy who could be anywhere, look like anyone, and doesn't have any sort of record." She pressed her hands together. "And to think, I was having such a great day."

"There has to be *some* way to track this guy, right?" asked Mon-El. "Fingerprints, bodily fluids . . ."

"You want to roam the city looking for places he peed? Be my guest." Supergirl gestured to the door.

J'onn shook a finger at Mon-El. "Mon-El might actually be onto something."

Mon-El, who'd been pinching Supergirl's side, straightened up and smiled. "I might?"

"How did Faust know where to find the artifacts he now

has in his possession?" asked J'onn. "Maybe they have a magical signature. If we can figure out that signature, we can track them to him."

Tlaca snapped her fingers. "Dark matter! Jason said the artifacts all contain dark matter."

A memory triggered in Supergirl's brain. Lena, at the gala, talking about her . . .

"Lena Luthor has a dark matter detector!" Supergirl exclaimed. Tlaca regarded Supergirl curiously, and she hastened to add, "Lena and I are friends, and she . . ." Supergirl chose her words carefully. "She mentioned meeting a guy who fit Faust's description at a talk she gave on dark matter. What if Faust used Lena—"

"To get to her dark matter detector," finished Alex.

Mon-El scratched his head. "So . . . Faust used the detector to track the Jar of Calythos to National City, and then used Tlaca's TV appearance to track the jar specifically to her?"

"Bingo," said Supergirl.

J'onn pointed at Supergirl. "Speak with Ms. Luthor and learn everything she knows about Faust. Then see if she can use the detector to locate him *and* the last artifact. Alex, get Agent Schott back here. Something tells me we'll need his technical expertise."

The Danvers sisters nodded.

"I'll stop by the library, too, and pick up some demonology books," said Supergirl. "We'll need to know more about these Demons Three."

"Perhaps I should contact Jason," said Tlaca. "This is turning into a bigger dilemma than I imagined. And he may have the information we seek."

Normally, Supergirl might've agreed, but Jason *had* told Tlaca to reach out to Supergirl, no doubt because she'd dealt with demons before and had the know-how to deal with them. There wasn't any reason to cause Jason strife while he was locating the Bell of Ulthool.

Supergirl placed a hand on Tlaca's arm. "Don't bother him just yet. We can handle this. You're working with an ace enforcement team."

One of the female recruits wandered up the stairs. "We're ready to train again, Agent Danvers."

"No, you're not." Alex placed a comms device in one ear. "Your sidearm isn't secured."

The recruit glanced down. "It's plastic."

"I didn't ask what it was made of. I said it wasn't secured." Alex tapped her comms and turned away, missing the dirty look the recruit threw at her. "Winn? We need you back at the DEO."

Mon-El snuck up behind the female recruit and snatched

the plastic sidearm from her holster. "And just like that you're dead," he said, pointing it at her. "*That's* why you secure it."

Blushing crimson, the recruit grabbed the sidearm and holstered it.

Alex turned back around with a scowl. "Winn, I don't care if you're almost at the front of the ice cream line."

"It may be a fake sidearm now, Recruit Parker," J'onn informed the young woman, "but we can't have that happening with a real one. Better to build the habit now."

"Yes, Director Henshaw." Recruit Parker snapped the strap across her plastic sidearm.

Alex rolled her eyes, still talking into her comms. "You said it was James's birthday *last* week when you left early to play miniature golf."

J'onn tapped a comms in his own ear. "Agent Schott, if you aren't at the DEO in fifteen minutes, you'll have all the time in the world to stand in ice cream lines . . . because you won't be working here."

Supergirl smiled at Tlaca, who looked more concerned with each comment. "We really do have this under control," Supergirl assured her. "And we'll find Faust."

Tlaca smiled back, but it was a troubled smile. "I am sure you can find him. I just hope you can do it in time."

3

JAMES OLSEN ENVIED SHORT PEOPLE. It was so much easier for them to go undetected in a surveillance van when they slid down in the passenger seat. All he got for his troubles was a backache and leg cramps from pressing his knees against the dashboard. For the phone call he was making, though, it was necessary. If his best friend Winn found out who was on the line, it was all over.

James popped his head up to check on Winn's progress in the FroZone queue, but Winn had stepped away and was shouting into his cell phone, waving his free hand.

"Jimmy?" James's mother spoke in his ear. "I asked you a question."

James slouched in his seat again. "Sorry, Ma, I got distracted. What'd you ask?"

"When are you coming home? It'd be nice if my CEO son could take a break once in a while and visit his mother."

"I know. Sorry," James apologized again. "It's been crazy around here," he said.

And he meant it.

When he'd lived in Metropolis, James had been the *Daily Planet*'s lead photographer and Superman's sidekick. Life had been fairly laid-back. But in National City, between being CatCo's acting CEO and helping Supergirl and the DEO *and* patrolling the city as Guardian at night, James barely had time for himself, let alone other people.

Maybe he noticed it more because he was constantly fighting it, but crime in National City was way higher than in Metropolis. And it was always rising.

The thought was kind of depressing.

"Well, how about I come see you, then?" asked Mrs. Olsen.

"You want to come here?" James repeated, sitting upright. "I don't think that's a good idea, Ma. Have you been watching the news about National City lately?"

"Of course! That Supergirl is amazing. I want to meet her! You know her, right?"

James nodded. "I do, but she's not the only hero in National City. Guardian is making a pretty big name for himself, too."

"Guardian . . . Guardian . . . I don't know him."

"I'm sure you've seen him on the news," James said. "He wears a knight's helmet and body armor with a shield that pops out of his sleeve."

"Oh, that sounds adorable," Mrs. Olsen said.

James rubbed a hand over his shaven head. "No, Ma, Guardian is not adorable."

The passenger door flew open, and James jumped in his seat, looking over at a starry-eyed Winn.

"Are you talking to your mom?" Winn asked, the lower half of his face one huge smile. He stepped onto the sideboard and craned his neck to shout into the mouthpiece of James's phone. "Hi, Mrs. Olsen!"

And just like that, James's one-on-one time with his mom was all over.

Since Winn had been abandoned by *his* mother, and his father was a murderous psychopath, James couldn't deny his best friend the chance to talk with someone parental.

So, with a sigh, he put his mom on speakerphone.

Mrs. Olsen was chuckling. "Hello, Winn, sweetheart. Did you get that sweater I sent?"

"I'm wearing it right now!" Winn grinned and tugged at the front. "It's my official stakeout sweater."

As soon as the words left his mouth, Winn seemed to realize they were the wrong ones.

His grin dropped, James's eyebrows shot up, and the line went quiet.

"Stakeout?" Mrs. Olsen repeated with no less than 100 percent attitude in her voice.

Winn chuckled. "Whaaat?" His voice hit a pitch reserved for opera singers. Winn cleared his throat. "Bad connection. No, I said it's my *takeout* sweater. I wear this all the time when I . . . uh . . . order Chinese food." He flinched and mouthed an apology to James.

"Take me off speaker, son," said Mrs. Olsen.

James's heart skipped a beat, but he did as he was told. Winn sucked in his breath and crept around to the driver's side of the van.

"I know what I heard," Mrs. Olsen informed James. "Now, promise me you two aren't doing anything reckless."

Technically, at that very second, they weren't.

"I promise," James said.

"And promise me you're leaving the crime-fighting to the superheroes."

Guardian was a superhero.

"I promise."

Mrs. Olsen's voice took on its usual loving tone. "All right then. What do you two boys have planned besides Chinese food?"

"Just picking up some ice cream," James said as Winn pulled away from the curb.

James glanced at Winn, whose hands were full of steering wheel and empty of ice cream. James prodded his friend, who arched an eyebrow and nodded at James's phone.

"Uh . . . we're at the front of the line now, Ma," James lied. "I have to let you go."

"All right, honey. But think about what I said about visiting. I miss you!"

"I'll think about it," James promised. "And I miss you, too, Ma. Love you." He ended the call and swiveled in his seat to face Winn. "Dude."

Winn held up a finger. "No, no, no. I do not want to hear it. I just spent twenty minutes in a line *outside*, waiting for ice cream." He looked at James. "Outside. Where the nature is."

"And yet you did not *get* ice cream," James pointed out. "What gives?"

"We have to get back to the DEO. Something big is going down, and they need all hands on deck. Well . . . they need *these* hands on deck." Winn wiggled his fingers.

"Why? What's happening?" James asked.

"Apparently, there's an evil magician on the loose," said Winn.

"Evil magician?" James wrinkled his forehead. "What, like the bad guy from *Harry Potter*?"

Winn tilted his head. "Mm . . . technically, Voldemort is a wizard."

James rolled his eyes. "All right, so what's up with the evil magician?"

"Alex said he's looking for a bell." Winn turned the steering wheel, and the van rounded a corner.

"A bell? I thought magicians were into rabbits," James said. "Why a bell?"

Winn shrugged. "I dunno. They're easier to clean up after? They make more noise when you shake 'em?"

James stared at him. "I really hope you didn't have pets as a kid."

"Relax! I'm kidding," Winn glanced in the side-view mirror as he changed lanes. "Hey, so, you told your mom you were going to think about something. What was it?"

"Oh, she wants to come visit"—James flicked his wrist absentmindedly—"but I told her it's not a good idea. Too dangerous."

Winn snorted and stopped at a red light. "Too dangerous? We have Supergirl to protect us."

James smacked his palm on the armrest of his seat and scowled at Winn.

"Wha . . . in *addition* to Guardian!" Winn amended. "You didn't let me finish."

Static sounded from the back of the van, followed by a woman's voice over the police scanner. "All available units in the area, we've got a robbery in progress at eight-two-five Mandrake. Homeowners say suspect is unarmed but commanding what they believe to be a . . . um . . . dragon."

James and Winn looked at each other.

A chirping sounded over the police scanner, followed by a man's voice. "Unit thirteen here. Can you repeat? It sounded like you said a dragon?"

"Ten-four. Fire and EMS are also en route."

"OK, we can be a few minutes late to the DEO for a *dragon*." Winn pulled to the side of the road and glanced at James. "What do you say, Guardian?"

James unclipped his seat belt. "Time to suit up."

While James got into costume, another call came over the police scanner.

"All units, all units, we've got a robbery in progress at seven-oh-six Mandrake."

"Isn't that across the street from the first break-in?" asked Winn.

"Yeah, it is." Guardian donned his helmet. "Let's see what's going on out there."

He straddled a motorcycle that was latched to the van floor and kicked loose the clasp.

Winn threw open the van doors and pressed a wall-mounted button. "Bombs away," he said as the ramp dropped.

Guardian revved the bike's engine and, with a squeal of tires and cloud of exhaust, took off. He could hear Winn coughing in his comms.

"Thanks for the lung cancer, Showboat," Winn said.

"Anytime." Guardian banked hard right on the corner and shot up Mandrake.

"You're not going to believe this," Winn said over his comms a few minutes later, "but I just heard about *another* robbery on the police scanner. This one at six-five-eight Mandrake. Weird thing is . . . from the looks of the security cameras, the place is empty. Someone made it in and out of there *fast*."

"A speedster?" asked Guardian.

He, Winn, and Supergirl were all friends with Barry Allen, a speedster code-named Flash from a parallel Earth, so Guardian knew such people existed.

"I don't think so," said Winn. "Just . . . be careful. I'm liking this situation less and less."

"With these robberies one after the other, it sounds

like a crew working their way down the street," Guardian replied. "Find out what's so special about the area."

"Ooh! There's a twenty-four-hour yogurt shop!"

"More special than that, Winn."

Guardian leaned low over the bike and opened the throttle, heading for the dragon-threatened house. No red-and-blue police lights flashed on the street, which meant he was first on the scene. When Guardian dismounted his bike and ran inside, however, he found the owners righting overturned furniture and refilling emptied drawers.

At the sight of Guardian, they gasped, but he raised his hands nonthreateningly.

"I'm here to help. I heard you'd had trouble." He cocked his head to one side. "With a dragon."

A woman in a bathrobe hurried forward. "I know it sounds crazy, but I swear it was here!" she said. "And then suddenly, it vanished."

"A vanishing dragon?" Winn spoke in Guardian's ear. "Sounds like something a *magician* might conjure."

"One that was good at illusions," Guardian agreed out loud.

The woman shook her head. "No, this thing was real! I felt the ground shake when it walked. I felt the heat of its breath."

Guardian watched a teenage boy put his video games

back on the shelf. "What did the thief take?" Guardian asked.

"Nothing!" The woman held her arms open. "I mean, I'm relieved, don't get me wrong. We're not rich, but we have—"

"Meredith!" a man shouted at her. "Don't tell masked vigilantes our business!" He gestured to Guardian.

"Nice," Winn said in Guardian's ear. "We're happy to help, grateful citizens."

"Have a good night, folks," Guardian told them, ignoring Winn. "And stay safe."

Guardian trotted down the stairs. "I'm headed for seven-oh-six now. Hopefully we'll find something more promising there."

"Don't bother," said Winn over the clacking of keys. "The owner responded to his security company and said nothing was taken."

"On to the next one then." Guardian pulled his motorcycle up to 658 Mandrake, which turned out to be a pottery store. As he stepped through the shattered doorframe, his boots crunched on glass *and* porcelain. While the glass debris diminished the farther he got from the entrance, the porcelain pieces increased in volume. He scanned the store's shelves, all of which were now empty, their contents smashed on the floor and slowly being ground under Guardian's boots.

"Eesh. No wonder Pottery Barn switched to selling furniture," Winn said in Guardian's ear.

"Someone deliberately broke these," said Guardian.

"How much do you want to bet it was our missing magician, looking for the bell?"

"You might be right," Guardian replied, approaching the manager's office. "I . . . what was that?"

A low rumbling down one of the aisles drew his attention. Guardian turned and followed the sound.

"Winn, who or what is in here with me?" Guardian whispered.

"What are you talking about?" asked Winn. "I told you that the place is empty—WHOA! James, get out of there now!"

"What? Why?" Guardian backed up, deploying his shield. "What is it?"

"Something you're *very* ill-equipped to face without a fire extinguisher." The panic was rising in Winn's voice. "You found the dragon!"

Suddenly, the interior of the pottery store was alight with orange flames.

Guardian crouched and raised his shield, feeling the heat all the way through his suit. As the fire died, he saw its source: a green, lizard-like creature that filled the space from floor to ten-foot ceiling with its presence.

The dragon screeched and took a floor-shaking step toward Guardian.

"That's my cue to leave," he said, sprinting toward the storefront.

"Wait a minute, wait a minute. You can't!" said Winn. "There's someone trapped in the store office."

Guardian skidded to a halt. "What?"

"I just saw movement in the office."

Guardian growled and whirled around. "You and I need to talk about what the word 'empty' means."

"It's pitch-black inside!" Winn said defensively. "I didn't notice until they lit up their phone."

After a few calming breaths, Guardian doubled back. He chanced a glimpse at the dragon, but it had thankfully stomped away to explore another aisle.

Guardian pressed his face close to the office door. "Is someone there?" he asked as loudly as he dared.

"Yes! Help!" A woman's muffled voice carried through from inside, and the door handle jiggled. "He locked me in here!"

"Guardian, watch your back!" Winn shouted in his ear.

Guardian turned as the dragon lashed its tail, leaping just before the tail connected.

Unfortunately, he didn't predict the tail making a return trip.

Guardian's feet were swept out from under him and he flopped onto his back.

"James!" Winn shouted.

"I'm good," he said, coughing.

But when Guardian sat up, he realized that wasn't quite true.

The dragon, feeling its tail strike something, had circled back around. It was now advancing on Guardian and slowly widening its jaws.

"Your armor is only heatproof to five hundred Fahrenheit," Winn warned as Guardian got to his feet. "If that thing gets any closer . . ."

"I won't let it." Guardian thrust out his right arm and clenched his fist. A grappling hook shot from his wrist-mounted holster and wrapped around a display rack next to the dragon.

Digging his heels into the floor, Guardian jerked on the grappling hook's line. With a creak, the rack tipped over, falling on the dragon . . . and then falling through it. The dragon continued to stand there with a display rack through its torso.

"Wait. What?" asked Winn.

James removed his helmet and stared in awe. "It's not real." He approached the dragon, ignoring the tinny sound of Winn yelling from inside the helmet.

The dragon spewed a stream of fire, but this time, James felt nothing. Then, without so much as a screech, the dragon disappeared.

James put his helmet back on. "Winn, the dragon isn't real. The heat, the fire . . . none of it."

"You couldn't have figured that out with your helmet *on?*" Winn's voice sounded almost hysterical.

A pounding came from the office door, and Guardian trotted over.

"Almost forgot." In a louder voice, he said, "Stand clear!"

He lifted his right leg and kicked out hard, knocking the door loose from its hinges.

Guardian stepped into the office, where a woman cowered in the corner.

"Is it over?" she asked in a quavering voice.

Guardian nodded. "You're safe now." He offered her a hand up. "Any idea what the person who did this was looking for?"

The woman wrapped her arms around herself. "Uh . . . yeah." She sniffled and wiped at her face. "He mentioned something about a bell. A special bell."

"That's our magician, all right." Winn's voice was in Guardian's ear again. "Also, I've been analyzing the area. The people here call it Little Bohemia, and it appears to be the nose ring capital of the world. It's also a hot spot for magic practitioners."

Guardian turned away from the woman and trotted toward the exit. "If that's the case, I'm guessing this won't be the magician's last stop of the night," he told Winn.

"I'll contact NCPD," Winn said. "And then we really need to get to the DEO."

"I'm on my way to the van," Guardian said, hopping onto the bike and shaking his head.

Real dragon or no, his mom *definitely* wasn't coming to National City anytime soon.

4

ALEX CREPT ALONG THE FLOOR OF the training simulator, darkness draped around her like a cloak. On either side, she could hear the rustle of pant legs, palms peeling off the floor, and myriad other sounds that were undetectable in everyday life but glaringly obvious in a silent maneuver operation.

The original goal had been for the recruits to get from the far wall to the observation deck without being tagged by a blindfolded Alex, but after she successfully caught every recruit, they deemed the task impossible. Now Alex was joining their ranks, trying not to get caught herself, while J'onn took over Alex's role. Since they had time before Winn's arrival, Alex hadn't wanted to waste any of it that could be devoted to training.

Especially since it was clearly needed.

The recruits were so intent on being silent that they weren't aware of the sounds around them. J'onn was making no efforts at stealth, so if the recruits paused and listened, they'd know when to remain completely still and avoid . . .

"Recruit Gibson, you're out." J'onn's voice carried from the far side of the room.

Several of the recruits near Alex decided to use his distance to their advantage. They sped up their crawling, walking, slithering . . . all rushing forward and raising a racket in their efforts to reach the observation deck before J'onn called their names. Alex sighed inwardly. It was never a good idea to underestimate a Green Martian.

J'onn was on the recruits in seconds, shouting name after name, each time met with groans and stomps off the simulator floor. *That* was what Alex took advantage of. With the noise level elevated, she shifted to her feet and leaped from toe to toe in wide-legged strides, reaching the observation deck and climbing to the top while J'onn called out another name.

When the last recruit was caught, Alex pressed a button on the control panel, and the lights switched on. The recruits and J'onn looked up at her, though J'onn was the only one smiling.

"It *can* be done," Alex declared. "You just need to work

on how you move and when you move. Tomorrow, I'll be providing each of you with a stealth—"

A voice from an overhead speaker cut her off.

"Director Henshaw? Agent Danvers? Supergirl's on her way back with intel," said Agent Vasquez.

"Already?" Alex checked her watch. Only twenty minutes had passed. "That was quick."

"We're on our way," said J'onn. "Agent Vasquez, come relieve us and begin the next training module."

"Yes, sir."

"The rest of you take five while we switch out trainers," J'onn told the recruits, who trotted off to grab their water bottles. He beckoned to Alex, and she descended the ladder to join him.

"Very impressive, the way you snuck past me," J'onn said when she reached the floor.

"You forget I was once a teenage rebel." Alex smiled winsomely at him as they left the simulator. "We excel at sneaking."

J'onn grinned and leaned in confidentially. "I hate to be the one to tell you, but parents *always* know when their children are sneaking about. My daughters could never get past me."

Alex paused for a beat, her smile widening. "It's nice to hear you talk about them."

J'onn, the sole surviving Green Martian, rarely spoke of his family. They'd been snatched from him hundreds of years ago in a genocidal move by the White Martians. When J'onn *did* mention his children, it was in solemn moments, so Alex was glad to hear him speak of them with amusement.

At Alex's comment, J'onn rubbed his knuckles thoughtfully against his chin. "I suppose they, and my wife, have been on my mind lately. Back on Mars, we'd be celebrating *Fihzpa'ak*, Family Week, right about now. With games and feasts and crystal crowns."

"Wow. Sounds very elegant," Alex said as they strode up the hall.

"It was," J'onn said. "Until the moment we'd smash the crystal crowns and use the largest shards for a knife fight to the death."

Alex lurched to a stop, and J'onn chuckled. "I'm *joking*, Alex. We'd use the smashed crystals for a spectacular light show."

She narrowed her eyes good-naturedly and continued up the hall. "Well, we may not have crystal crowns here, but we can definitely party and feast as soon as we've dealt with Faust."

J'onn nodded. "Any word from Maggie on him?"

"Let me—" Alex reached toward her back pocket and

stopped. "Shoot, I left my phone on the observation deck. Be right back."

"I'll meet you in the control room," J'onn said as they parted ways.

Alex retraced her steps and opened the simulator door to laughter.

"All I can say is . . . thank *God* we get a break from Dictator Danvers." Recruit Parker's voice carried to the doorway.

Alex stopped and pressed her back against the wall, staying out of sight.

"Hear, hear!" chorused several female voices.

"May the reign of Dictator Danvers soon endeth!" declared Recruit Espinoza.

Alex frowned. Were they talking about *her*?

Several people laughed.

"First of all, you're a huge nerd." A male voice, Recruit Gibson's, spoke up, his words greeted with giggles. "Second of all, Danvers isn't that bad."

All the girls groaned.

"Of course you'd say that. You're one of her pets!" said Espinoza. "She's way easier on the guys."

Alex had heard enough. Coughing loudly, she entered the simulator room. Instantly, the rebellious recruits (who numbered *way* more than Alex liked) quieted and scrambled to their feet.

Alex strode past them. "Don't bother," she said. "That's an order from your dictator."

Behind her, she could hear the recruits shuffling and fidgeting, but she didn't dare turn and let them see how scarlet her face had become.

Alex shimmied up the ladder and grabbed her phone, unlocking it to find a message from Maggie.

Hey, babe! No leads on Faust. I know you said he could change his appearance. Did Kara notice any tics of his when she met him?

Tics? Alex texted back. *Like facial twitches?*

LOL. Like habits or mannerisms. Gestures he keeps repeating. He might look different, but his habits won't change. And while he's under duress, they'll crop up more.

Oh, good idea! Alex texted. *I'll check with Kara. Thanks for the help! xoxo*

If I hear anything new, I'll let you know. xoxo

Alex squeezed her phone, sending Maggie a long-distance hug, and pocketed the device before clambering back down the ladder.

"Agent Danvers?" Recruit Espinoza was waiting for her at the bottom. "We . . . we didn't mean what we said."

"Sure you did," Alex replied. "You just didn't think you'd get caught. And now you're trying to save your job."

Espinoza's nostrils flared but she pressed her lips together and breathed deeply. "Ma'am . . ."

"The world is tougher than I am, Espinoza." Alex pointed to Parker and the other recruits. "And if you and your pity party can't handle *this*, you won't survive a day in the field."

Espinoza didn't answer, so Alex turned and walked away. She was almost to the door when Espinoza called, "Ma'am? Do I . . . do I get to keep my job?"

All the recruits' eyes were on Alex as she pivoted to face Espinoza. "That is an excellent question." Alex held up an index finger. "A better question, for *all* of you, is, if I can't count on you to have my back, do you think you *deserve* to keep your job?"

Without waiting for a response, Alex opened the door and walked out. Only when the door had fully shut behind her did she let her lower lip tremble.

Welcome back to high school, she thought.

When she was a teenager in Midvale, kids had teased Alex for having a "weird" sister: Kara. If anyone made fun of Kara now, Alex could simply apply a gentle chokehold until they apologized, but it was different when the attacks were about Alex herself. She could fire back, as she'd done at the recruits, but their verbal barbs still stayed under her skin.

Alex took a deep, calming breath before marching toward the control room, almost colliding with J'onn at the top of the stairs.

"God!" she said, raising her hands. "Sorry, J'onn."

"No harm done. I was just coming to look for you." J'onn took in her miserable expression and frowned. "Is everything all right?"

"Sure. Yeah." Alex wrinkled her forehead. "I just . . ." She chewed her lip. "Do you think I'm a dictator?"

J'onn's eyebrows went up. "A dictator? No." He crossed his arms. "Why do you ask?"

She gestured at the lower level behind her. "Some of the recruits are calling me . . . Dictator Danvers," Alex said sheepishly.

J'onn relaxed his arms. "I see." Instead of getting upset, he grinned. "Do you know what the police force on Mars used to call me? *Lanua ka'or J'onzz.*" He chuckled. "Roughly translated, it means 'Tearjerker J'onzz.' Because I always made the new officers cry."

"OK, but you actually *made* people cry, so it's an accurate nickname." Alex put her hands on her hips. "I don't *feel* like I'm a dictator."

J'onn shrugged. "Then ask the recruits what the issue is."

"No." Alex swatted away the idea. "If I act like I care, it gives them power over me."

"So, instead you'll let this anger fester?" J'onn rolled his eyes. "Sounds healthy."

A flash of red and blue caught Alex's attention as Supergirl arrived with an armload of books.

"I can't worry about this right now," Alex said. "We have to find Faust." She walked over to her sister, who was handing the books to Mon-El and Tlaca.

"Here you go," Supergirl said. "All sections related to the Demons Three, the artifacts, and *Homo magi* are marked."

"You found all these *and* talked to Lena in twenty minutes?" Mon-El marveled.

"Well, I *am* Supergirl," she teased with a wink.

"What'd you learn from Lena?" Alex asked.

"Faust is definitely still in town." Supergirl faced Alex. "I spoke with Lena—who was *not* happy to learn his true colors, by the way—and she showed me her dark matter detector. Despite its name, that stuff is glowing nice and bright in National City."

J'onn nodded his approval. "Where, exactly?"

Supergirl shrugged. "That's the problem. The detector's meant to search vast regions of space, so it can only zoom in so close. We can see dark matter glowing in National City, but anything more precise is impossible."

"Wait a minute," said Alex. "If the dark matter detector can find Faust, can't we use it to find the Bell of Ulthool?"

Tlaca glanced up from a book she and Mon-El were poring over. "Would that work?"

"I already thought of that," said Supergirl. "But the

only location on Earth that showed dark matter was here. National City."

Alex narrowed her eyes. "That doesn't make sense. Could the bell be in a parallel universe?"

"Not according to this." Mon-El held up the book. "All the artifacts are bound to *this* Earth."

"Faust has two of the artifacts here." J'onn stroked his chin. "What if the third is here in National City, as well?"

"If you're talking about that very special bell, it *is*." Winn hurried up the control room steps with James. "You're not gonna believe what we saw on patrol." He held up a tablet computer.

J'onn, Alex, Supergirl, Mon-El, and Tlaca gathered around the tablet, peering at the image on-screen.

Winn and James glanced at Tlaca with quizzical expressions.

"Uh . . . does anyone else see the tall lady in the gold dress?" Winn jerked a thumb in Tlaca's direction.

"Right! Winn and James, meet Tlaca." Alex gestured at the princess, who offered her hand to the newcomers. "She's helping us with our latest crisis."

"What are we looking at, Agent Schott?" J'onn asked, studying the tablet. "Security camera footage?"

"Of Guardian and a new little friend he made," said Winn. He tilted his head to one side. "Don't they play well together?"

Supergirl squinted and then widened her eyes. "Is that a dragon?"

"What?" Mon-El snatched the tablet from Winn. "Supergirl, you said there *weren't* any on this planet! I threw away my rider's license and everything!"

Winn pointed at Mon-El. "OK, you and I are gonna revisit *that* statement later, because the nerd in me is losing his mind."

Alex snickered. "The *nerd* in you? Like there's anything else?" she teased.

Winn gave her a withering look. "I am also two percent interested in watching other people eat competitively, thank you." He turned to Mon-El. "But no, ordinarily there aren't dragons here."

"That thing is made of magic," added James, taking the tablet back from Mon-El. "Some guy was using it to chase people away while he ransacked their homes and stores. We thought he might be your missing magician."

Alex and Supergirl looked at each other. "Faust," they said in unison.

"Faust? That's his whole name?" Winn scoffed. "Not 'the Phenomenal Faust' or 'Faust the Fabulous'?" He spread his hands open in the air before him, making an invisible marquis.

"He's Felix Faust, and he's not *that* kind of magician,"

said Supergirl. "He's an evil little turd who can conjure illusions and wants to unleash demons on the world," she finished with a scowl.

Then Supergirl and Alex told Winn and James about the museum and Tlaca and the Flame of Life and the artifacts. When Alex mentioned the Bell of Ulthool, James and Winn shared a look.

"Our mystery man was after a bell, too. It's either a really big coincidence, or the same guy," James said.

"You were right." Alex glanced at J'onn. "All the artifacts *are* here. Which means we have to get to the Bell of Ulthool before Faust."

"Or we have to get to Faust before he finds it," said Supergirl. "At this point, I'd be happy with either outcome."

Winn headed for his desk. "What's Faust's first name? I'll check—"

"We already did. There's nothing," said Alex. "And don't bother looking for his face. He can create illusions, so he can look like anyone."

"Yeah, but not just illusions," said James. "That dragon might have been made of magic, but it was plenty real at first."

J'onn frowned. "What do you mean 'at first'?"

"I could feel the heat of its breath and I could feel the floor shake when it walked," James explained.

"Maybe you were having a psychosomatic reaction," Alex mused. Before she'd joined the DEO, she'd been on a med school track and had seen patients with symptoms like what James described. "If certain areas of the brain are triggered, you can *think* you feel a particular sensation. People have even been known to feel limbs itch after they've been amputated. They're called phantom sensations."

"I'd agree with that if the dragon hadn't knocked me over with its tail," James replied. He sped up the security footage Winn had captured and showed them.

James, dressed as Guardian, was pressed close to a door, the dragon behind him. A moment later, the dragon swung its tail and, in a shower of blue sparks, laid Guardian out on his back.

"Ooh!" said Alex and Supergirl, wincing.

"I'm impressed," said J'onn as they saw Guardian spring to his feet. "A shot like that would've knocked anyone else out."

James didn't respond. Instead, he stared at the video and frowned.

"James?" Mon-El nudged him.

"Something's not right." James dragged his finger across the tablet screen to rewind the footage. They watched again as the dragon swung its tail. James paused the footage just as the dragon's tail struck him.

"Right there." He pointed. "Those blue sparks did *not* happen."

"Are you certain?" asked J'onn. "In the moment, you might have been too much in shock to register them."

James let the video play, and this time Alex stopped it.

"Do you see *that*?" she asked, tracing her finger over the screen.

Faint blue flecks flitted away from James and toward the exit. They might've been mistaken for bad pixilation on the screen if the path they followed wasn't so direct.

"Yeah. What is that?" asked Supergirl.

"Magic." Tlaca spoke up. "Only special security cameras will capture it." She pointed at the footage. "Those blue flecks would belong to a magician. My guess is Faust was casting an invisibility illusion over himself."

"So *he* tripped me up as he was running away," said James with a nod. "Not the dragon."

"Clever," said Alex. "And everything else *was* just phantom sensations."

"That shop's in a neighborhood called Little Bohemia," Winn explained from his desk. "Apparently, the people around there are known for practicing magic."

Alex held the tablet up for Winn to see. "Can you track something like this?"

"If I had the original camera that could capture magic

so I could figure out how it works, sure," he said with a nod.

"Where was this footage taken?" Supergirl asked James.

"Six-fifty-eight Mandrake. The owner—" James started to say, but Supergirl had already zipped out to the balcony.

"While she's doing that, Winn, can you start monitoring citywide alerts?" Alex asked. "Any one of them could be Faust."

Winn's eyebrows almost disappeared into his hairline. "The *whole* city? But I'm just one man. One overworked, under-caffeinated, ice cream–deprived man."

"This could be a good task for the recruits," said J'onn. "They've been working on tactical maneuvers. Maybe it's time for a little surveillance work."

At the mention of the recruits, Alex stiffened, but she nodded and pressed an intercom button. "Agent Vasquez? Could you bring the recruits to the control room, please?"

"Yes, ma'am," came the response a moment later.

"Hey, this might be something," said Winn. "There's been a break-in at one of the suites in Plastino Plaza. The registered guest is Princess Tlaca M . . . Mito . . . tiqui?" He rolled away from his computer. "Wait. Tlaca. Is that you?" He spun in his seat to gape at Tlaca with wide eyes. "Are you a princess?"

"I think you're focusing on the wrong part," James told him as all heads swiveled in Tlaca's direction.

The princess clutched a hand to her chest. "Someone broke into my room?"

Alex gave her a sympathetic look. "I'm guessing Faust thinks you have the other artifact."

"No! Just paperwork for my charity. And some donations I gathered at the gala." Tlaca brought her hands to her mouth. "Oh, the donations . . ."

J'onn looked to Mon-El. "Can you—"

"Go with her to the hotel?" He nodded. "Of course." Mon-El offered an encouraging smile and an arm to Tlaca. "I've been told you're pretty good at flying. *I'm* pretty good at hanging on tight."

Tlaca barely smiled back, her forehead a mass of worry lines. "Please. Let us hurry. Before this night gets any worse."

"Agent Schott," said J'onn as Mon-El and Tlaca headed toward the balcony, "can you find out when that hotel break-in was reported and access nearby cameras at that time?"

"*Can* I?" Winn scoffed. "Is the Space Pope reptilian?" At the confused look from J'onn, Winn raised his eyebrows. "*Futurama*? The . . . never mind. I'm on it." He turned to his keyboard.

Agent Vasquez bustled up the steps with the recruits. "Director Henshaw, where do you want them?"

Alex waited for J'onn to issue orders, but when she looked at him, he gestured to her.

"Take it away, Agent Danvers."

Alex curled her lip but faced the recruits.

"Recruits, you've seen the control room and run simulations here. Now you're looking for an actual suspect," said Alex. She fixed each recruit with a stare, daring them to defy her, or to say one mean thing against her. With J'onn and her other friends present, Alex felt stronger and more confident.

"This man who calls himself Felix Faust, among other aliases, is virtually untrackable at the moment, which means all we can do is monitor citywide alerts." Alex motioned to the desks but didn't take her eyes off the recruits. "Find an empty station and get to work. When you spot a break-in or burglary, report it to me or Director Henshaw. That is all."

Alex turned away with a lift of her chin. There was no way anyone could see anything dictator-like about *that*.

Even so, she noticed James leaning against a pillar and giving her a strange look.

"Is there a problem?" she asked, walking over to him.

James blinked rapidly and smiled. "Funny. I was going to ask the same thing." He lowered his voice. "Why were you giving all your recruits the stink eye?"

Alex scowled. "I wasn't. I was showing them who's in charge."

"They *know* who's in charge," he said. "You don't need to pound your chest and do a gorilla roar."

Alex raised an eyebrow. "Since when did you become an expert on military leadership?"

James laughed. "I'm not, but I *am* the CEO of a media empire. Intimidation only goes so far before people stop seeing you as their leader and start seeing you as something else."

Alex could almost see the word "dictator" forming on his lips.

"Well, you're wrong. That's not what's happening," Alex informed him. She strode toward the balcony to indicate the conversation was closed.

As Alex reached the top step, Supergirl landed on the railing, camera in hand.

"The Faust Finder 5000 has been acquired," she said with a grin.

"Let's track this guy down," Alex said. "I could use something to punch."

5

"ARE YOU ALMOST DONE?" SUPER-girl peered over Winn's shoulder as he typed the world's longest algorithm into his computer.

Winn scoffed. "Uh . . . considering I *just* learned magic is traceable and you *just* brought me the tracing device, I think a little patience is in order." He wrinkled his nose. "I also think you've had enough sour cream and chive potato chips." He moved the bag out of Supergirl's reach.

"Sorry." Supergirl straightened and breathed into her hand. "All I had for dinner was two pot stickers. Hey, what's this?" She picked up a legal pad that had been under the chip bag. Winn's sloppy handwriting filled the top page, along with a doodle of an old-fashioned, blue telephone booth.

"No, that's . . . !" Winn snatched the legal pad from

Supergirl's fingers. "That's not something for you to worry about. Just a side project." He slipped the legal pad into his desk drawer.

"You know I have X-ray vision, right?" Supergirl crossed her arms.

Winn sighed wearily. "Fine. It's my Doctor Who fanfic, OK?" His cheeks flushed pink. "I'm working on an adventure where he's stuck in the Ghost Quadrant with a bunch of convicts."

"I see." Supergirl nodded slowly, trying to hide a smile. "And is the . . . uh . . . Ghost Quadrant anything like the Phantom Zone where *I* was stuck with a bunch of convicts?"

Winn scowled at her. "I said it was fanfic, Kara. I didn't say it was *good* fanfic." He waved a dismissive hand. "Now, leave me to my shame and algorithms. Shoo! Shoo!"

Supergirl strolled away with a chuckle, then looked up at the video wall, which displayed a map of National City. Every burglary and home invasion in the last hour had been marked with a glowing red dot, but so far, none of the incidents had involved a perpetrator in a purple suit. And Winn's scan of Plastino Plaza after the break-in hadn't proved fruitful, either.

"Man, it'd be nice if we had something or *someone* concrete to look for," Supergirl said.

"Maggie gave me a helpful tip earlier." Alex joined her.

"I know you only spent a few minutes with Faust, but did he have any tells . . . any gestures he kept doing that seemed a little off?"

Supergirl squinted thoughtfully. "Nooo. I mean, he kept tucking his hand into his jacket like he was Napoleon, but I think that was just a pride thing."

"OK, well, it's worth considering. Not many people pose like nineteenth-century emperors these days," Alex said with an amused smile.

Supergirl smiled, too. Her phone vibrated in her boot, and she pulled it out to see a message from Mon-El.

Is it OK if I give Tlaca directions back to the DEO?

She showed the message to J'onn, who reluctantly nodded. "We're going to need her help. And with so many visitors coming through, I'm thinking of turning this place into a theme park anyway," he muttered.

"Hey, if you do, I want a roller coaster named after me!" Winn swiveled his chair to face J'onn. "And it has to be a *good* coaster, not a lame kiddie one where you only scream when the car catches on fire."

"Winn?" Alex spun his chair back to face his computer. "I will name a whole park after you if you get that algorithm finished."

"OK, OK."

While Winn returned to work, Supergirl texted Mon-El.

A minute later, there was a whooshing sound from the balcony as Tlaca and Mon-El appeared.

"That was fast," Supergirl commented as she walked over to greet them. "Were you hovering around the corner?"

"Celebrating with coffee downstairs, actually." Mon-El held out a paper bag. "And I brought you a cruller. Figured you might be hungry."

Supergirl took it with a gleeful gasp. "Food! You are *the best*." She planted a kiss on his cheek and led the way back to the control room, peeling apart the spirals of the cruller. "What were you celebrating?"

"My hotel room was ransacked but none of my things were stolen," said Tlaca.

"Oh, right, I heard about the break-in!" Supergirl turned to the princess and spoke around a mouthful of pastry. "I'm sorry Faust violated your privacy."

Tlaca snorted. "My life has not been private for many years. One of the downsides of being a public figure. You understand, no doubt."

Supergirl chewed her cruller and nodded mechanically. Thanks to the DEO and her connection to the media world, she'd been lucky enough to maintain a secret identity. And since Kara Danvers wasn't a particularly glamorous one, nobody gave her a second glance.

"How's the search coming?" Mon-El asked.

"Winn's almost finished with the algorithm," Supergirl said. "We're hoping for good news any—"

"Done!" Winn shouted, raising both hands in the air. "With a lovely magic hot spot around National City Music Hall, whose silent alarm was tripped two minutes ago." He fired finger guns at the screen.

"Nice work, Agent Schott!" said J'onn. "Remind me to give you a raise."

"I could also use a company car," Winn suggested.

"Don't push it."

National City Music Hall, Supergirl repeated to herself. *Come for the music, stay for the mayhem . . . again.*

When National City had been reverted to Ancient Rome, the Villain of the Week had turned the concert hall into his own palatial estate. The place had been a funhouse of magic and madness.

It looked like it was time for more of both.

"OK, since Tlaca and I can fly, why don't we take Guardian and Mon-El there now?" Supergirl asked. She faced Tlaca. "If you still want to be involved, of course."

Tlaca nodded firmly. "I would love nothing more than to retrieve those artifacts and bring Faust to justice."

Supergirl turned to Alex and J'onn, neither of whom seemed enthused about her plan.

"What's wrong?" she asked.

"Why don't you wait for us to assemble a strike team?" asked Alex. "Then we can all go together."

Supergirl knew she had to choose her next words carefully. As the only person in the room who remembered dealing with Marcus and his magical menagerie, she was the best equipped to face whatever Faust threw at them. Plus, Tlaca, a *Homo magi* like Faust, would be with her, so it made sense for them to clear the way for the strike team.

"We don't really know how much longer Faust will be at the music hall," Supergirl said. "We should act on this as soon as possible."

Alex pressed her lips together. "What about taking *other* people who might be able to fly?" Her eyes flitted to J'onn, but Supergirl shook her head.

In the fight against Marcus, there had been a lot of fire involved, and J'onn, who had a dark past with it, had frozen up a bit. Between that potential threat and Tlaca's actual fireballs, Supergirl didn't think it wise.

But, of course, she couldn't say that.

"Let's not play all of our cards just yet," she said instead. "Besides, I think the four of us can handle Faust until the rest of the team gets there."

"All right," J'onn agreed, holding up a hand when Alex started to protest. "We'll see you there soon."

"Mon-El, Guardian?" Supergirl turned to her friends.

James scooped up his helmet and put it on, already zipped into his Guardian costume. "Let's do this." He faced Tlaca. "I hope you're a better pilot than Supergirl."

"Hey! I've gotten you everywhere in one piece," Supergirl retorted.

Tlaca smiled and ushered Guardian toward the balcony. "There are no snacks on this flight, but it will be smooth," she replied.

Supergirl and Mon-El followed, Supergirl wrapping an arm around her boyfriend.

"Ready?" she asked.

"Up, up, and away," he said.

They zipped across town and touched down outside National City Music Hall, where two police cruisers were already parked.

"We'll handle this one," Supergirl told one of the cops. "He's kind of a trickster."

The officer nodded. "We'll be here if you need us."

Supergirl wrenched open the front doors of the music hall, and strobe lights flashed overhead, indicating activation of the silent alarm. Using her X-ray vision, Supergirl peered across the foyer and into the auditorium. Faust was there, still in his purple suit, checking under each seat on one of the balconies.

Nodding to her companions, Supergirl strode across the foyer and threw open the auditorium doors.

"Felix Faust!" Supergirl leaped into the air and hovered in front of his balcony.

Faust straightened up, stared at Supergirl, and then grinned charmingly. "*Supergirl*. You're not upset with me for running off earlier, are you?" He batted his eyelashes.

"That depends." Supergirl crossed her arms. "Are you willing to hand over the Wheel of Nyorlath and the Jar of Calythos?"

"You know about them? Good for you!" Faust clapped the fingertips of one hand against the palm of the other. He approached the balcony. "I'm guessing *she* told you?" He nodded down at Tlaca, who sprang into the air.

"You messed with the wrong woman," she informed him with clenched fists. "When I am done with you, your body will be so covered in bruises, no one will know where your suit stops and you begin."

Faust tucked his hand into his jacket and gawked at Supergirl. "Are you going to let her talk to me like that?"

Supergirl extended her hand, palm up. "The artifacts. Now."

Faust held her gaze for a moment. Then he leaned his elbows on the balcony and sighed. "I love a good opera, don't you?"

"Faust . . ." Supergirl wriggled the fingers of her extended hand, still hovering before him. "The agents coming to get you won't be as nice as I am," she warned.

"The music is so moving," Faust continued, as if she hadn't spoken. "You can almost picture the scene that goes with it." He stroked his chin, eyeing both Supergirl and Tlaca. "Of course, if you have actresses to play in them, why not go *that* route?"

He flicked his wrist, and a spear appeared in Supergirl's hand, while a sword appeared in Tlaca's.

Tlaca chuckled ruefully. "You have made a *grave* mistake in giving me this." She raised her weapon.

"It's just an illusion with phantom sensations," Supergirl reminded her. "You—WHOA!" Her head drooped with the weight of a helmet that had suddenly settled on her head. She reached up and felt wings springing from either side. Supergirl turned to Tlaca, who was wearing the same helmet . . . a Viking helmet.

Faust peered down at Guardian and Mon-El, who were poised to fight.

"Normally, the roles for this scene fall to women," said Faust, "but in these modern times, who cares about gender?" He flicked his wrist at Guardian and Mon-El, and they were made over in the same Viking treatment. "Now for a little mood music."

Faust snapped his fingers and a familiar stringed intro filled the music hall: Wagner's "Ride of the Valkyries."

"Is he serious?" Tlaca asked.

"Uh . . . guys?" Mon-El shouted. "What's going on?"

"*That's* it!" Supergirl told Faust. "You had your chance." She tossed aside the spear, which vanished, and grabbed Faust by the front of his suit jacket, hauling him over the balcony railing.

"OK, OK, I can see how you might consider me a threat." Faust chuckled nervously and clutched his jacket closed with both hands. "But shouldn't you be more worried about my minions?" He tilted his head and lowered his gaze to the floor.

Supergirl looked down, too, and almost dropped Faust.

All three doorways of the auditorium were filled with screaming, cackling, gray-skinned creatures. Stretched to their full heights, they would've towered over Guardian and Mon-El, but the creatures were hunched over to better peer at Guardian and Mon-El through wide, pitch-black eyes.

"Wow, the ushers here are *not* attractive," Mon-El said, taking a step toward Guardian.

"I think they want to do more than show us to our seats," Guardian replied.

As if to confirm his suspicions, one of the creatures emitted an ear-piercing screech and raised a pitchfork in the air, lightning arcing from tine to tine. The creatures in the other doorways charged into the room, and Mon-El and Guardian readied themselves for a fight.

Instantly, Tlaca dove down to help them while "Ride of the Valkyries" slid into its trombone intro.

Despite his precarious position, Faust clapped with glee. "It's just like I imagined it!" he exclaimed.

Supergirl tightened her grip on his jacket. Somehow, she found it doubtful he'd imagined a princess in a Viking helmet hurling fireballs at a demon in a downtown theater.

"Let's go," she told him.

"Aren't you worried about your friends?" Faust asked, pointing below. He clucked his tongue. "Can they really survive an onslaught of demons without you?"

As much as she hated humoring Faust, Supergirl stole a glance at her friends. Guardian was swinging across the auditorium on grappling wire. He bashed a demon between the shoulders with his shield while another demon fired a hail of brimstone at him from its claws. Four other demons had Mon-El on his back and were struggling to pin him down, driving knees and elbows into his face and other pressure points. Tlaca wrestled in midair with a winged demon, and neither of them seemed willing to back down.

"My friends can handle themselves," Supergirl said as Mon-El flung the demons from him and sprang to his feet. "Now let's—"

The rest of Supergirl's sentence was cut off as lightning surged through her body. Every appendage seized and then relaxed, her fingers losing their grip on Faust, who half fell, half jumped to the theater aisle below. Supergirl glared at the pitchfork-wielding demon who'd attacked her, firing a blast of heat vision at its weapon. The pitchfork glowed bright red but continued to arc electricity.

"Maybe I should watch from somewhere a little less . . . busy." Faust sprinted toward the stage.

Supergirl clenched her jaw and considered giving chase, but she couldn't afford to turn her back on the kilowatt-crazed demon.

It cackled and pointed its pitchfork at Supergirl, bolts of electricity streaking toward her. Supergirl darted toward the ceiling, but the demon followed her path with the pitchfork, and the electricity found its endpoint.

"Supergirl!" Mon-El shouted as she tumbled through the air. He zipped across the auditorium, fist extended, and knocked the pitchfork-wielding demon to the front of the room, its weapon skidding into the orchestra pit.

Unfortunately, he couldn't attack the demon *and* catch the Girl of Steel. She struck the theater floor with a *BOOM!*, obliterating the carpet beneath her and leaving a Supergirl-sized dent in the concrete.

Shaking off the static in her system, Supergirl leaped up

to see the winged demon choking Mon-El with one clawed hand. She glanced back at Guardian, who'd picked up a crowd control stanchion and turned it into a club. He'd laid out two of the demons but was coughing and staggering amid a cloud of black smoke. Tlaca lay near him, the coils of a hissing black viper wrapped tight around her struggling form.

"Winn, tell me Alex and J'onn are en route!" Supergirl shouted before throwing herself at the winged demon holding Mon-El.

"Whaaat are you talking about?" asked Winn. "They're already there."

"What?" Supergirl blasted the demon's hand with her heat vision. It screeched and backhanded Supergirl, knocking her into a row of seats. "Where are they?"

"At the risk of sounding like a horror film cliché . . . they're right behind you."

Supergirl climbed into the air and studied the scene. The winged demon dodged a punch from Mon-El and kneed him in the stomach. The demon who'd zapped Supergirl was crawling into the orchestra pit to retrieve its weapon. "How many agents came with them?"

"Uh . . . eight," Winn responded.

Supergirl's eyes darted from one demon to the next. Four knocked out by Guardian and Mon-El, two fighting to keep Tlaca on the floor, and two running toward Supergirl.

Her gaze shifted to Faust, who was sitting cross-legged on the stage, enthralled by the show.

"That sneaky purple . . ." Supergirl gritted her teeth. "Winn, count to five and then tell Alex it's me."

"What?"

"Just do it!"

Supergirl dove into the orchestra pit and snatched up the demon with the lightning pitchfork. The demon kicked and struggled against her until Supergirl dropped it on one of the balconies overlooking the stage. When she heard the buzz of Winn's voice, she nodded at the demon.

The demon who she was pretty sure was Alex.

Supergirl had hoped for a nod of understanding in return. Instead, the demon snarled and primed its pitchfork.

"Ha-haaaa!" Faust clapped, beaming up at the balcony. "Someone's in for quite a shock!"

"Alex, don't!" Supergirl shielded herself with her arms as the demon raised its weapon.

At the very last second, the demon swung its pitchfork away, pointing it at the stage.

Faust stopped clapping. "Oh, cr—"

Electricity shot from the pitchfork, striking Faust square in the chest. He flailed, gurgled, and then fell backward.

"Someone's in for a shock all right," Supergirl heard Alex say.

Supergirl grinned and faced her sister, who was back to her usual, glorious human self. Alex looked Supergirl over and sighed with relief.

"Oh, thank God." She wrapped her arms around Supergirl. "I'm not saying I *wouldn't* love you if you were a harpy, but . . . we'd probably have to rethink the family Christmas photo."

"What?" Supergirl chuckled and pulled away. "You saw me as a harpy? Faust had Tlaca and me seeing ourselves as Valkyries."

"Ohhh." Alex nodded. "'Ride of the Valkyries.' Makes sense now." She winced. "Listen, I'm sorry I shot you. A couple of times." She held up her laser pistol.

"Are you kidding?" Supergirl asked. "I'm glad I didn't use my heat vision on you like I did on—" Her jaw dropped. "J'onn!" Supergirl leaped down from the balcony to find the DEO director supervising Faust's arrest.

He glanced over his shoulder at Supergirl and smirked. "Supergirl! I should write you up for assaulting a superior officer." J'onn displayed the back of his hand, which was marred with a black scorch mark.

Supergirl rushed over, fingers to her lips. "J'onn, I am *so* sorry. Are you OK?"

"I'm fine," he said, chuckling. "And I'm very lucky Mon-El can take a hit."

The two men clasped hands.

"*And* a choke," Mon-El reminded him. He nodded past Supergirl. "But that's not nearly as impressive as Alex surviving an across-the-room punch."

Alex swatted the air. "I barely felt it." With a grin, she added, "Plus, it helps that I'm wearing shock-absorbing battle armor." She pounded on her chest.

"Are you *all* wearing it?" Supergirl looked up the aisle to the agents Tlaca and Guardian had been fighting with. She was relieved to see one of the agents cutting through the rope that bound Tlaca while a couple of others helped Guardian onto a stretcher.

"Every member of the strike team is alive," J'onn assured her. "A little bruised and embarrassed, but still happy to call this operation a success."

He, Supergirl, Alex, and Mon-El watched the arresting agents drag Faust across the stage.

"Supergirl, I think it's wisest for you and me to fly Faust to the DEO as quickly as possible," said J'onn.

She nodded her confirmation.

"What do we do when Faust wakes up?" Alex asked. "He could turn us all against one another again."

"Is there a way to block his magic?" asked Mon-El.

But when the DEO team took the question to Tlaca, she shook her head.

"Not without knowing its source," she said. "I can

create a magic lock for whatever cell you put him in, though."

Supergirl bit her lip. "Not trying to poke holes, but didn't he find a way through the magic lock on your bracelet?"

Tlaca nodded. "If his cell is magically locked by two people, however, it will take two people to unlock it." She looked at J'onn. "I will just need one of your agents to forge the other lock."

"I'll do it," said Mon-El, raising his hand. "Magic sounds cool."

Tlaca nodded her approval. "You look hearty enough to survive a blood sacrifice."

Mon-El lowered his hand. "Sorry, what was that?"

"A joke." Tlaca smirked at him before turning to J'onn. "It may take some time to forge the lock. Can you keep Faust under control until then?"

"Forget under control. We can keep him unconscious," Supergirl said, blowing on her knuckles.

J'onn pushed her hand down. "We can manage," he told Tlaca.

"And you can *fly*," she said, giving him an appraising look. "Or was that also an illusion of Faust's?"

J'onn smiled. "It's no illusion." He nodded to the DEO agents holding Faust, and they brought him forward.

"We'll see you back at the DEO." J'onn transformed into his true form, Martian Manhunter, and grabbed Faust under one arm while Supergirl took the other.

As they flew from the music hall, she overheard Mon-El ask Tlaca, "So am I going to get a wand?"

Supergirl smiled, but it didn't stick. What J'onn had said was true: The operation to capture Faust was a success.

But where, she wondered, were the stolen artifacts?

6

WHERE ARE THE ARTIFACTS?

It was the first question on a long list Kara had written to ask Faust when he woke up. She'd left the illusionist in the DEO's care for the night so she could prep for her interview with Tlaca, who, as far as she knew, still had no idea Supergirl and Kara Danvers were one and the same. After the battle at the music hall, Kara had worried Tlaca might cancel their interview, but the next morning when Kara called to confirm, the princess was still eager to meet.

Now, as Kara sat in one of CatCo's conference rooms with a notepad and tape recorder, she was finding it difficult to switch from Girl of Steel to Girl of Story.

How did you break through Tlaca's spell? Kara jotted down the question for Faust on her notepad.

"Danvers." Snapper's voice wasn't loud *or* angry, but Kara still broke the tip off her pencil in surprise.

"Yes, Chief?" She looked up, adjusting her glasses.

"I'm not sure when I became your secretary, but you have a visitor." He beckoned to someone behind the door, and Tlaca appeared in a gold jumpsuit and oversized sunglasses.

"Princess Tlaca," Snapper announced. As he strolled away, he tossed a couple of words at Kara: "Wheeler-Nicholson."

Tlaca raised an eyebrow at Kara, who had offered her hand in greeting. "What is Wheeler-Nicholson?"

My boss's not-so-subtle way of reminding me to get award-winning news from you, Kara thought.

She waved Tlaca's question away. "Nothing. Thank you for coming in!" She shook the princess's hand. "I know you're busy."

"You do not know the half of it," Tlaca said with a chuckle. "Even away from home, I am working to fix some problem or another."

Kara nodded, knowing Tlaca was referring to Faust. "I hope everything works out."

"It will. As long as the government stays out of the way

from this point forward. You know how their officials can be, I am sure." She winked at Kara as if they were sharing some inside joke. "Always causing trouble."

Government officials? Kara thought. *Does she mean the DEO? Supergirl?*

"Yes. Right." Kara adjusted her glasses and poised her pencil over her steno pad. "So, we know you're a problem solver. Why don't you tell me more about yourself, Tlaca . . . er . . . Princess Tlaca?" she corrected with a smile.

"Well . . . I grew up in a small village outside Monterrey in Mexico," Tlaca began. "I was lucky enough to be born into wealth and privilege, my father being the village leader. But I couldn't help noticing those around me who suffered."

Kara couldn't help noticing that Tlaca steered clear of mentioning her magical roots.

She cleared her throat. "Unless I'm wrong, I think there might be something supernatural about you, as well?" Kara leaned closer. "I saw the fireballs at the museum gala."

Also, I was hit by one, she added to herself.

Tlaca sighed. "Yes, and I am afraid that situation did not play out as I expected. The man I attacked was a criminal, you see, but because Supergirl chose to defend him, *I* appear as the bad guy, when in fact, *Supergirl* let him—"

Kara smacked her pencil against the table. "Yep, I get it!

You think Supergirl screwed up." Her harsh tone surprised even her, and Kara pressed her lips together. "Sorry," she said, taking in Tlaca's startled expression.

Tlaca pushed back her chair and stood. "I think maybe this was a mistake."

"No, no!" Kara jumped up, too. "I am *truly* sorry. We're just . . . very big Supergirl fans in National City."

Tlaca eyed her but didn't move.

"Please." Kara gestured to the chair. "We don't have to talk about Supergirl or the gala. Tell me about The Forgotten."

To Kara's relief, Tlaca nodded and took her seat once more.

"I worked first for the Mexican government, trying to get funding reappropriated for those in need," Tlaca said. "Many have no choice but to leave their homeland and their families to find work in the United States. And while it is admirable that my people strive for greater things in a land of opportunity, the farther south you travel in Mexico—to Guerrero, Oaxaca, or Chiapas—there is *no* opportunity and much poverty."

Kara tilted her head as she wrote. "Oaxaca I've heard of, but not the other two."

Tlaca nodded sadly. "Most people haven't, even though they are brimming with Aztec and Mayan culture. The population is largely indigenous peoples who still speak the tongue of their ancestors. But they are isolated by the mountains around them and overlooked by . . . well . . . everyone."

"That's where *you* come in." Kara gestured to Tlaca, who nodded.

"My organization, The Forgotten, provides funding for education and infrastructure across the mountains. I've traveled from Metropolis to Opal City to Gotham to . . . well, you saw me last time I was here." Tlaca smiled at Kara. "All to meet with heads of state and request donations. And now I speak to you, hoping to reach the general population."

"My article can definitely do that. In National City, at least," Kara agreed. "Our readership is in the millions. If I cover the plight of The Forgotten, I'm sure plenty of people would love to help your cause."

Tlaca held up a finger. "And if each of those readers donated just one dollar, think how much The Forgotten would benefit!"

Kara and Tlaca spoke for half an hour more, Tlaca filling Kara in on the specifics of The Forgotten's endeavors. When they'd finished talking, Kara flipped through her notes and nodded in satisfaction.

"I think this will be more than enough. Thank you." She stood and shook the princess's hand once more. "And I'll contact you before the article runs to make sure I've got all the facts straight."

"Wonderful." Tlaca pressed Kara's hand between hers. "Thank you, Miss Danvers."

After Kara walked Tlaca to the elevator, she strode triumphantly to Snapper's desk, dropping her steno pad on it with a satisfied smack.

Snapper looked down. "There better be a dead spider under there. I can't imagine another reason for so much noise and wind."

"*That*," Kara informed him, "is the source material for my award-winning article on The Forgotten."

She began telling Snapper about the Tlaca interview, leaving out the Supergirl bit, but the longer she spoke, the more frown lines gathered on Snapper's face.

"So, if we . . ." Kara faltered at his expression. "If we . . . um . . . OK, *why* are you starting to look like a shar-pei?" she finally asked with an exasperated sigh.

"What you're describing isn't an article, Danvers," Snapper replied. "It's a very long newspaper ad."

Kara made a face. "What? No, it's not!" she scoffed. "It's the story of a woman who wants to use her money—"

"*Her* money?"

"Fine. Hers and other people's," Kara corrected. "To improve the quality of life for the forgotten."

"And if you call with your donation now, we'll also throw in a set of steak knives," Snapper finished.

Kara took a deep breath and clenched her fists.

"I'm not writing an ad," Kara said in an even tone. "I'm trying to raise awareness about The Forgotten. That's what I *do* as a reporter!" She couldn't help throwing her hands in the air. "I raise awareness."

Snapper didn't appear impressed. "You can do that just as easily with some cans of spray paint and a brick wall. Your job is to inform, educate, and entertain, Danvers. This article you're planning doesn't hit that final note."

Kara fought the urge to roll her eyes. Snapper was talking to her as if she'd never written an article in her life. As if she hadn't earned a Wheeler-Nicholson nod. She knew she couldn't tell Snapper her career was going fine without his advice, but somehow the thought found its way to her face.

"What's with the glowering stare?" Snapper asked, meeting it with a scowl of his own. "You don't like what I have to say?"

Kara took a deep breath. "Boss, I don't mean to be argumentative—"

"You always mean to be argumentative," Snapper replied.

Kara forced a tight smile. "But don't you think I've learned a thing or two about reporting?"

"Don't you think *I've* learned a thing or two?" Snapper gestured to himself. "I'm not talking just to hear myself,

Danvers. I'm trying to help you." Snapper shook the steno pad at Kara. "Now take this and go find a good story."

Kara growled inwardly but grabbed her steno pad.

"And take Miss Luthor with you," Snapper added.

"What?" Kara looked over her shoulder at Lena, who was striding toward Snapper's desk with a shopping bag in hand. Instantly, Kara's mood lifted.

"Hey, you!" She greeted Lena with a hug. "What brings you to CatCo?"

"This, actually." Lena held up the bag.

"Lena Luthor!" Kara grinned and took it from her. "Did you get me another present? You shouldn't—"

Kara froze when she saw what was inside: the gown and glasses she'd ditched at the gala to become Supergirl.

"I found them in the museum garden," said Lena. Her arms were now crossed, but she was grinning. "I'd *love* to hear how you got home without your dress. I didn't see any headlines about a blond girl running naked from the museum."

Kara clutched the bag to her and forced a laugh, steering Lena away from Snapper's desk. "Blond girl running . . . that's a good . . ." She fiddled with her glasses. "You know what happened? Those fireballs were flying everywhere, and I thought I smelled burning fabric." She held up the bag. "So, I yanked off the dress and borrowed some woman's coat to run for help. I must have left the glasses behind, too. I'm sorry, Lena," Kara finished with a wince.

Thankfully, Lena reached out and squeezed Kara's arm. "I'm just glad you made it out in one piece." She looked around and leaned closer to Kara. "Between us, it turns out my 'friend' Felix wasn't such a friend after all. Supergirl paid me a visit last night, looking for him."

Kara brought a hand to her mouth, feigning surprise. "No!"

Lena arched an eyebrow. "Apparently, Felix is some criminal mastermind who was using my dark matter detector to find mystical goods."

Kara shook her head. "Unbelievable. He seemed like such a nice guy." *That* wasn't acting on Kara's part; she was genuinely disappointed in Faust.

Lena shrugged and sighed. "Well, better to learn the truth now than later. Anyway, I can't stay, but I thought I'd swing by and ask about my dress." She nodded to the shopping bag.

"I'm actually on my way out, too. Story-chasing." Kara rolled her eyes in the direction of Snapper's desk. "*He* still wants me to talk to the richy-riches in town."

Lena clucked her tongue in disapproval. "Don't forget, there *are* other areas where you can find great story material. Technologyyy," she said in a singsong voice. "My offer to connect you with people still stands."

"Thanks," Kara said, "but if I don't humor Snapper and get at least *one* story from someone named . . . Emerald von Moneybags, I'll be looking for a new job."

Lena grinned. "Well, promise me you'll at least *consider* the tech angle, and I'll help with the other part." She reached into her purse and pulled out a credit card–sized sliver of platinum, stamped with the word EMPIRE. "Here. Don't lose this."

"Empire? What is it?" Kara took the card and flipped it over to find an address stamped on the back.

"A very exclusive club that caters to the wealthy and influential," said Lena. "You can bring a guest, and I suggest you do. That place is highly intimidating."

Kara pocketed the platinum and smiled gratefully at her best friend. "Thank you *so* much. I'll make all of this up to you somehow."

Lena waved her away. "You don't have to do that. It's what friends are for!"

Kara shook her head. "Nope, I mean it. If you *ever* need to borrow some sweatpants or my library card, I'm there. I will *make* sacrifices," she said in a mock serious voice.

Lena laughed. "How about a cup of coffee?"

"I can do that, too," Kara said, ushering Lena toward the elevators. "You can even have fancy sprinkles."

• • •

"Hey, do I look all right?" Mon-El flicked lint from the cuffs of his black, button-down DEO shirt.

"Perfect." Kara assured him with a smile. "You'll fit right in."

Mon-El nodded and tugged at the seat of his pants.

"Not so much when you do that," she said.

"Sorry," Mon-El replied. "It's these DEO-issued fancy pants." He laughed. "Hey, I just got that expression!"

"Good job." Kara smirked and glanced down. "What's wrong with the pants?"

"They're too tight. Like they were made for a child-sized man." Mon-El glanced back at the tag. "Are these Winn's?"

Kara chuckled. "If you'd like, I have something else you can wear." She reached into her journalism bag and pulled out the evening gown and glasses Lena had brought her.

"*So* funny." Mon-El tweaked Kara's nose and then kissed her. "Shall we?"

He quit fidgeting and stood tall, shifting Kara's hand to the crook of his elbow as they ascended the steps to the club entrance.

A silhouetted figure just inside pushed the door open for them, but when the man saw the club's latest visitors, he frowned.

"I'm sorry, but this is a private establishment," he said, jutting out his chin.

"That's why I have this." Kara held up Lena's platinum card.

The man took it from Kara and inspected it. "And you are . . ."

"Offended that you're asking." Mon-El mirrored the man's tone and posture. "Eric, isn't it?"

Kara glanced at Mon-El in surprise. So did the doorman.

"Well . . . yes," said Eric.

Mon-El beckoned for him to hand the platinum card back. "I've never had an issue with you before, Eric. In fact, I love the macarons you make for us every year." He narrowed his eyes. "I'd hate to see them *and* you go away."

Eric swallowed hard. "Yes, sir. My apologies. Welcome to Empire."

He stepped aside and beckoned Kara and Mon-El through the doors.

"Mon-El, how did you do that?" Kara whispered.

"I'm the former prince of Daxam," he said with a shrug. "The elite act the same on any planet."

Kara glanced back at Eric, who was mopping his brow with a handkerchief. "But how did you know who he was?"

"Oh, *that*." Mon-El grinned and showed Kara his cell phone. "I looked up the club on the way over here." He clicked a link labeled "Our Staff." Halfway down was a picture of Eric, the door attendant, with glowing accolades from club members.

"I love the macarons he makes for us every year," Kara read aloud. She stood on tiptoe and kissed Mon-El. "You never cease to amaze me."

"Thank you." He started to bow but frowned. "Nope. These pants aren't meant for that."

"OK, let's get you situated." Kara guided him into the first sitting room.

The polished wooden floors were accented with Persian rugs, tucked beneath marble-topped tables and leather armchairs. Most of the chairs were occupied by loud, boastful septuagenarians.

"You donated ten thousand? That's nothing," a man with an eye patch told another at his table. They sat with two others playing poker, the pile of money in the pot enough to cover Kara's rent for a year.

"What's wrong with ten thousand?" the man to his right asked. "It's far more than that research center deserves. I don't even like whales."

"So don't give your money away! You do enough of that here," the man with the eye patch teased, and his friends laughed. "It's to you, Glenn."

Glenn, the man to his left, was fast asleep in his armchair. At least, Kara *hoped* he was asleep.

"Glenn!" The man in the eye patch elbowed him, and Glenn snorted but kept sleeping. "Hey, tall, dark, and loitering." The man in the eye patch looked at Mon-El. "You any good at poker?"

Mon-El glanced at Kara and then at the man in the eye patch. "Poker? Yeah." His eyes flitted to the hundred-dollar bills on the table. "But I forgot my huge stack of money at home."

"It's all right, you can play with Glenn's. He was bound to lose it, anyway."

Bored, with money to burn. Definitely not for me, thought Kara.

Her life might be chaotic, but at least it had meaning.

"Uh . . ." Mon-El deferred to Kara, who smiled.

"It's all right," she told him. "I've got things to do."

A tinny voice sounded in her ear.

"Hey, Kara, are you at that fancy club yet?" Alex asked.

Kara pressed a hand to the comms button in her ear. "Just got here." She turned away from the poker players. "And let me tell you—OOH!"

She collided with a man carrying a mug of coffee. It spilled down the front of his shirt and he yelped.

"Oh, gosh! I'm so sorry!" Kara looked up at the man and sucked in her breath. "Really, truly, sorry."

She'd just bumped and burned Monocle Man.

"Kara?" Alex asked.

"Sorry, gotta let you go," Kara whispered, pressing her comms button.

Monocle Man scowled at Kara. "You're lucky my coffee wasn't hotter, or the lawsuit I'd slap you with would have you *working* at this club instead of roaming it."

Kara bit her lip and stepped back. "Let me find you a napkin."

But a butler was already bustling over, towel and seltzer in hand.

"Tell me," Monocle Man said as the butler dabbed at the coffee stain. "Do you make it a habit of following people around and crashing into them? Or am I just special?"

Kara shook her head. "No, sir. I just . . ." She thought back to the gala when Snapper had spoken to Monocle Man. If she wanted an award-winning story, she had to start somewhere. "I just wanted to hear about that pocket watch of yours," she said. "I'm Kara Danvers, and I write for *CatCo* magazine. At the museum gala, you told my boss the watch had an interesting story."

Monocle Man's scowl lessened slightly. "It belonged to my grandfather. He stole it from Harry Houdini."

That story Kara hadn't expected. And even though she'd never admit it to Snapper, it *was* interesting.

"He stole it from Harry Houdini, the magician?" she asked, reaching into her purse for her pen and steno pad.

"Houdini wasn't just a magician," said Monocle Man, his eyes aglow with admiration. "He was a stunt performer, an escape artist, a master illusionist, and one heck of a pickpocket."

The butler stepped away, and Monocle Man settled in an armchair. He gestured to an empty one beside him, and Kara sat, as well.

"A pickpocket?" Kara couldn't help but smile.

Monocle Man nodded. "Only with his friends, of course. He taught them a few tricks of his trade, and when my grandfather successfully nicked his watch, Houdini let him keep it." Monocle Man held up a finger. "As a matter of fact . . ."

He shifted in his seat and reached into a smashed, weathered wallet to extract a laminated black-and-white photo. No doubt he kept it close at hand to show off to anyone, whether they asked to see it or not.

"Oh, wow," said Kara, shifting closer.

"You see?" Monocle Man pointed to a young man who looked like him. "Here's my grandfather and his friends, and that one *there* is Houdini."

Kara smiled and gingerly took the photo from Monocle Man. She couldn't help thinking that Houdini looked a little like Maxwell Lord, one of her former nemeses. And the guy next to him looked a little like Faust.

Wait a minute.

Kara frowned and held the image closer.

He looked a *lot* like Faust.

Same goatee, same rakish grin . . . his suit was even a dark color, which could have very well been purple.

Kara flipped the photo over, but there was nothing on the back but a year: 1894. She turned the photo back over and pointed at the man resembling Faust. "Who was *this* man?"

Monocle Man peered closely. "Let me think . . . I believe his name was Faustenhammer. He wasn't into picking pockets, though. More of an illusionist and hypnotist."

"A hypnotist?" Kara's hand shook with a new realization, and she passed the photo back to Monocle Man before she crushed it. "Was his first name by any chance Felix?"

Monocle Man's eyes widened. "Why, yes! You know of him?"

"A little more every day," Kara said, getting to her feet. "Thank you for your time, Mr. . . ."

"Cheval," he supplied. "Jonathan Cheval."

"I'll come back to hear the rest of your story, Mr. Cheval," Kara promised him.

She tucked her notepad and pen away and hurried across the room to Mon-El's poker table. "We have to go."

Her words were greeted by a chorus of protests.

Mon-El indicated the cards in his hand. "But I've got—" He glanced up at Kara and, seeing the look on her face, immediately put the cards down. "Sorry, fellas. Duty calls."

The older men grumbled as he left the table, but Kara grabbed Mon-El's hand and sprinted toward the exit.

"Now we're *running*?" Mon-El tugged at his pants. "Kara, I'm about to invent the hundred-meter hobble. What's going on?"

"Faust," Kara said. "He's not just an illusionist." Kara tapped a comms button in her ear. "Alex?"

Nothing.

"Alex!"

Mon-El frowned and ushered Kara out the front door as Eric held it open. "Kara, what is it?"

"Faust isn't just an illusionist," she repeated. "He's a hypnotist, too." Kara set her jaw. "Which means everyone at the DEO could be in danger."

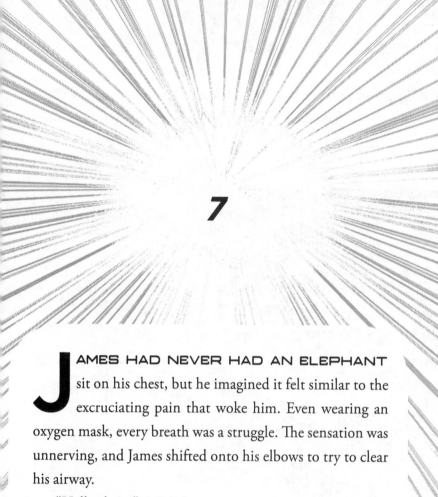

7

JAMES HAD NEVER HAD AN ELEPHANT sit on his chest, but he imagined it felt similar to the excruciating pain that woke him. Even wearing an oxygen mask, every breath was a struggle. The sensation was unnerving, and James shifted onto his elbows to try to clear his airway.

"Hello there!" A DEO nurse approached his cot. "How are you feeling?"

James peeled off the oxygen mask, wincing as it grazed his cheek. During the concert hall fight, his Guardian helmet had protected him from outside attacks, but it had also done its own damage, digging into his face after a particularly harsh blow. "What happened to me?"

The nurse tilted her head sympathetically. "You were

exposed to our latest and greatest anaerobic gas last night. As soon as it enters your lungs, it absorbs the oxygen in them and knocks you out." She handed James a plastic cup containing two pills. "It also gives you a killer headache, so I recommend ibuprofen."

"Did we at least get Faust?" he asked, swallowing the ibuprofen capsules.

"Oh yes," said the nurse. "I had to implant his inmate tracker when he was brought in last night."

"That's good." James flinched as pain arced across his temples. "When will I feel better?"

"When you start moving around," the nurse said. "The more oxygen you reintroduce into your system, the better."

James nodded and swung his feet onto the floor. As minimal as that exertion was, he still had to rest his hands on his knees.

"It'll get easier the more you move," the nurse promised. "I recommend a stroll up and down the hall."

James carefully shifted his weight to his feet and stumbled forward. The effort felt only slightly less Herculean than swinging his legs out of bed, but he inhaled deeply and pushed on. He poked his head into each infirmary room that he passed, looking for his friends, but he appeared to have been the only one incapacitated during the concert hall fight.

"Of course," James muttered to himself.

He wandered past the DEO break room, where a TV was tuned to CatCo's news station. A reporter was finishing a story about a slew of package bombs on the south side of National City. The story after that was about an arsonist targeting retirement homes.

At least we caught Faust, James thought. *That's one less criminal on the streets.*

Still, he wished that number was bigger. They needed a way to stop crime for good.

A shout from farther down the hall interrupted his thoughts. James glanced at the agents in the break room, but they continued to eat and chat, so he trotted off to investigate by himself, feeling a bit better with each step. As he neared the prison wing, James could finally make out what was being shouted. He could also make out *who* was shouting: Kara.

"Help! Someone get me out of here!" she cried.

"Kara?" James called, running toward the prison wing. He rounded the corner and lurched to a halt outside the second cell.

Kara, dressed as Supergirl, stood behind bullet-proof glass, pounding on it with all her might. She stopped when she saw him.

"Oh, thank God. Get me out!"

James rushed forward. "How did you get in here?"

Supergirl shook her head. "I was so stupid. Faust tricked me."

James pressed his hand on the biometric scanner outside the cell door. The scanner flashed green but the door didn't open. "It's not working. Can't you just bust through?"

Supergirl ran a hand through her hair. "No, the door's secured with magic locks, and it takes two people on the outside to unlock it."

"I'll get Alex," said James, pivoting on his heel to race back up the hall.

"No!" Supergirl slapped her palm against the glass.

James raised his eyebrows. *That* wasn't like Supergirl.

Supergirl's face took on a pained expression. "Please, don't tell anyone who was with us at the concert hall. I don't want them to know how badly I messed up."

"They're going to find out anyway," James countered.

She shook her head. "Not if we can catch Faust before they do. *Please.*"

That definitely wasn't like Supergirl. She wouldn't sneak something so huge past her friends. Supergirl always owned up to her mistakes. And after everything they knew about Faust, James highly doubted she'd let herself get tricked into entering his cell.

He also couldn't help noticing that Supergirl hadn't used his name once.

James nodded. "OK. I'll see if someone else can help."

"Look for one of the new recruits!" Supergirl shouted after him.

James jogged back up the hall, but instead of stopping at the break room, he continued to the control room, where J'onn, Alex, and Winn were talking.

"Since the artifacts Faust stole are probably drenched in his magic, which yes, sounds disgusting, I figure if we follow the magic, we find the artifacts," said Winn.

"Good thinking, Agent Schott," said J'onn. "James!" He greeted James with a clap on the back. "Glad to see you on your feet. How are you feeling?"

"Better the longer I'm awake." James managed a small smile. "Say, where's Kara?"

"She's at some private social club with Mon-El," said Alex. "Empire, I think it's called."

"I checked out the pictures on their website, and it is *swanky.*" Winn sang the last word. "I'm not even joking, they have a champagne vending machine."

James smiled. "How long have Kara and Mon-El been at the club?"

Alex glanced at her watch. "He left about five minutes ago to meet her. Why?"

"*Supergirl* is in Faust's holding cell." James raised an eyebrow. "Apparently, he trapped her there."

"Yeah, right. Like Kara's that gullible," said Winn.

Alex pressed a comms button in her ear. "Hey, Kara, are you at that fancy club yet?"

After a second, Alex nodded and gave a thumbs-up to the others. Then she winced.

"Kara?"

J'onn leaned close. "Is everything OK?"

Alex tapped her comms button. "Well, Kara's having an awkward moment, but she's definitely not downstairs."

"That's what I figured." James smirked. "I'll tell Faust 'Nice try.'"

He turned away, but Alex grabbed his arm.

"Wait a minute." She narrowed her eyes shrewdly. "Let's think this through."

J'onn crossed his arms. "Do you have an idea, Agent Danvers?"

"We put a tracker on all our inmates," Alex said. "What if we played along with 'Supergirl'"—Alex used air quotes—"and set her free but watched where she went?"

"You want to unleash Faust on National City?" Winn asked, wide-eyed. "The guy conjures dragons and harpies, not puppies and rainbows. And even if he *did* conjure puppies, they'd probably shoot lasers from their eyes."

"I'm afraid you've lost me, too," J'onn told Alex.

"I interrogated Faust earlier and he refused to give up

the location of the two artifacts he has," said Alex. "So why not let him *lead* us to them?"

James shook his head. "It's a good idea, but Winn's right. When Faust gets out of here, the first thing he's going to do is terrorize the city and tear it apart . . . literally . . . looking for the last artifact."

Alex picked up Winn's tablet. "Not if we tell him exactly where to find it."

Winn snorted. "OK, but we don't *know* where to find it."

"We don't have to," said Alex. "We feed Faust a fake location and tell him the Bell of Ulthool can't be accessed without the other artifacts present."

"Then we follow Faust and steal back the Wheel of Nyorlath and Jar of Calythos when he produces them." J'onn stroked his chin. "That just might work."

"Trick the trickster." James grinned. "I like it."

"Winn?" Alex turned to him. "Can you work up a fake location?"

"Already on it," he said, tapping away at his tablet.

Alex nudged James. "Ready to go free our prisoner?"

"Actually, SuperFaust begged me not to tell you," said James.

Winn snickered. "SuperFaust. Nice."

"So I'm going to grab one of the recruits instead," James finished.

Alex nodded. "Don't tell them the plan. We want Faust

to believe *we* see him as Supergirl, and the fewer people who know, the better."

James flashed a thumbs-up and hurried back down the hall to the break room, pointing at the first person he spotted in a recruit uniform. "Supergirl needs to see you."

The recruit looked up from the toaster pastry he was eating. "Me?" he asked, crumbs falling from his mouth.

"Let's go!" James snapped his fingers and gestured toward the door.

The recruit jumped up from his seat and followed James to the prison wing.

"Supergirl!" The recruit regarded her with wide eyes. "How did you end up in there?"

"Long story," she said, waving away his question. "I need each of you to say a different word. That'll unlock the door." Supergirl—or rather, Super*Faust*—pointed to James. "You say 'Open,' and you say, 'sesame.'"

James snorted. "Seriously?"

SuperFaust rolled his eyes. "Don't get me started."

James glanced at the recruit. "Open."

"Sesame."

The cell door slid to one side, and SuperFaust stepped into the hall with a sigh of relief.

"Thanks, guys. Time to go find Faust!" He pointed up the hall and sprinted away.

James followed, grinning to himself.

"Hey, team!" SuperFaust slowed to a stroll in the control room. "Any progress finding that last artifact?"

James elbowed him. "Aren't we supposed to be looking for Faust?" he whispered.

He and the DEO team couldn't give in *too* easily or they'd look suspicious.

SuperFaust leaned toward James. "If we find the artifact, we find him," he whispered back. In a louder voice, he asked, "So . . . the artifact?"

Winn approached with the tablet. "We've got good news and bad news. The good news is we know the location of the Bell of Ulthool." He pointed to a blip on the map that James recognized as a defunct tire factory.

"The bad news"—Alex held up one of the library books— "is that we need the other two artifacts to get it."

"What?" SuperFaust snatched the book from her. "Let me see."

Alarms went off in James's head, but when SuperFaust flipped through the book, Alex pointed to the text on an end page. No doubt it had been blank a few minutes ago, with Alex hastily adding new words.

"Right there. Apparently, whoever hid the Bell of Ulthool built in a fail-safe for it," Alex said. "And we can't get the other two artifacts because Faust won't tell us where he hid them."

SuperFaust smiled and tapped the page. "You're not gonna believe this, but I talked to him downstairs before he locked me up, and he told me where they are."

J'onn raised his eyebrows. "Really?"

Alex frowned. "How did you get him to talk when I couldn't?"

SuperFaust shrugged. "I guess I just have a way with people." He pointed toward the balcony. "Why don't I pick up Faust's artifacts and meet the rest of you where the Bell of Ulthool is hidden?"

"I'll come with you," said J'onn.

SuperFaust held up a hand. "No need, John. The rest of you should stay and try to track down Faust."

James's first instinct was to comment on the mispronunciation of J'onn's name, but he pressed his lips together. Correcting Faust might put him on the defensive.

Alex rested a hand on SuperFaust's arm. "Be careful."

SuperFaust smiled. "I will be."

He strode up the balcony steps, and the other DEO members exchanged a triumphant glance.

"Oh, one more thing," SuperFaust said, turning around. "Keep an eye on the time, won't you?"

With the flick of his wrist, a pocket watch the size of a wrecking ball appeared between SuperFaust and everyone else in the control room. It swung side to side in swift, swooping arcs. Left, right. Left, right. Side to side.

"What . . ." James's eyes were entranced by the watch, and further words failed him.

In his peripheral vision, he could see Alex and Winn frozen in place, too, but the longer he focused on the watch, the less he cared.

SuperFaust chuckled and strolled down the balcony steps toward the DEO members.

"How *stupid* do you think I am?" he asked, his voice deepening as his features returned to those of Faust. "Supergirl pronounces J'onn's name wrong and *none* of her friends correct her?"

Faust paused in front of James. "I *could* kill all of you, but I'm in a generous mood. Plus, I don't want to miss *Lunchtime with Laurie*." He rubbed his hands together. "She's holding a séance with Ben Franklin today! I've always wanted to ask about his kite."

James blinked but said nothing, thought nothing.

"Instead, I'll do you all a favor," Faust continued. "One that will make you see just what I intend to do with the power of the Demons Three." He pressed his fingertips together and softened his voice, walking from person to person. "You feel tired. You want to sit down."

James bent his knees and dropped to the floor. So did Alex and Winn.

"Yes, very good," said Faust. "Your eyelids feel heavy. You want to close them."

The world went dark as James's eyelids slid shut.

"When I snap my fingers," Faust murmured, "you will open your eyes and be in your ideal world, and the Demons Three will give you *exactly* what you deserve."

Silence.

SNAP!

Alex entered the training simulator with a smile on her face. She couldn't explain why, but for some reason, everything just felt . . . better. The recruits were already engaged in a mock firefight, using every technique she'd taught them. Upon seeing her, they all stood at attention.

"At ease," she told them, strolling among the ranks. "I'm impressed at your initiative to practice on your own!"

The recruits grinned at one another.

"We're nowhere near combat ready," said Recruit Parker. "And if we're going up against someone like Faust—"

"No." Alex shook her head. "Faust is extremely dangerous. Leave him to the seasoned agents."

"Yes, ma'am," said Recruit Parker. "Thank you for looking out for us, ma'am. We know you only want what's best for us."

"That's absolutely right," said Alex, marveling at how understanding the recruits suddenly were. "Did Director Henshaw talk to all of you, by any chance?"

"No, ma'am," Recruit Jessup replied. "Why?"

Alex smiled. "No reason. Let's run a fast rope insertion. Parker, why don't you take point?"

In a city of skyscrapers, the DEO team occasionally had to rappel from helicopters to enter a combat situation quickly.

"Me, ma'am?" Recruit Parker stepped forward. "But I've never led air before. Only ground."

Alex gestured to the simulation floor. "Which is why you should practice."

Recruit Parker nodded and called ground versus air positions to her classmates. Alex climbed to the top of the observation deck, Recruit Parker and the airborne recruits climbed a twelve-foot tower, and the remaining recruits took hiding places on the ground.

"Time starts . . . now," Alex said, clicking a stopwatch.

Recruit Parker, Recruit Espinoza, and five of their classmates tied on harnesses, latched themselves to rappelling ropes, and began their descent while ground recruits fired lights from their laser pistols. Once the airborne team reached the floor, Alex called, "Too slow! You should be able to tie your harnesses in less than two minutes. Run it again. Parker, make it happen."

"Yes, ma'am!" Recruit Parker gathered her team, and they climbed to the top of the tower once more, undoing their harnesses to start from scratch.

"Time starts . . . now!" Alex shouted.

Again, the recruits harnessed and rappelled, but again their time was too slow.

"Parker! Every second you delay a landing is another second you're sitting ducks!" Alex barked. "You will practice until you get it right!"

"Yes, ma'am!"

Up the recruits went to the tower. Alex couldn't help feeling relieved at how little pushback she was getting. The recruits were following her instructions without question.

"Time starts . . . now!"

The recruits raced to harness themselves and latch in. But this time, when they began their descent, Recruit Parker didn't rappel.

She fell.

It wasn't a long drop, but far enough that Alex heard something snap when Parker hit the floor.

"Parker!" Alex gripped the sides of the observation deck ladder and slid down, sprinting toward her recruit as soon as her boots touched concrete.

Recruit Parker was rolling from side to side, clutching her lower leg. "I'm . . . guessing we didn't make it in time," she grunted.

Alex chuckled weakly. "No, you're a little over, I'm afraid. How does your head feel?" Alex pulled a flashlight from a cargo pocket and shone it in Recruit Parker's eyes.

"Fine. I didn't hit it." Recruit Parker shifted to a sitting position and leaned against Alex, hoisting herself onto her one good leg.

"Wait, whoa, where are you going?" Alex ducked under Recruit Parker's arm.

"Again," said Recruit Parker through clenched teeth. She pointed to the ladder, and her teammates began to climb. Recruit Parker twisted away from Alex and hopped after them.

Alex stared, dumbfounded for a moment, before coming to her senses. "Recruit Parker, stand down!" She shook her head. "Better yet, *sit* down!"

Recruit Parker let her good leg crumple beneath her as she settled on the floor.

Alex grabbed a med kit and knelt beside her. "What on earth were you thinking just now?" she asked, wrapping an emergency blanket around the shivering recruit.

"We have to practice until we get it right," replied Recruit Parker.

"Not when you're injured, you don't." Alex shook her head. "And how did you fall, anyway? I've seen you tie a Swiss seat. You're a wiz with a harness."

Recruit Parker smiled at the praise. "Recruit Espinoza was having trouble with *her* harness, and we were running behind, so I helped her and didn't tie mine." She gazed up at Alex. "You wanted us to make it in time."

"Parker . . ." Alex was at a loss for words. "I also want you to make it in one piece."

She pulled the mobile scanner from the med kit and ran it over Recruit Parker's leg. As the damage showed on-screen, Alex grimaced.

"Looks like you fractured your tibia. Your shinbone," she added at a confused look from Recruit Parker. "You're lucky it wasn't worse."

Recruit Parker smiled. "You're right! I *am* lucky."

Alex scrutinized her. "Do you really feel that way? Or are you saying it for my sake?"

"No." Recruit Parker shook her head vehemently. "I'm lucky to have made it into the training program *and* that you're so much tougher on the women. I know it's because you care."

"Exactly!" Alex clapped a hand on Recruit Parker's leg, and the woman fought back a cry of pain. "Oh, sorry! I can give you something for that." Alex winced and rummaged through the med kit.

"This should make you feel better *and* give you some hard-earned rest." She injected the recruit's leg with a pain-killer, and the woman visibly relaxed.

"Thank you," Recruit Parker murmured.

Alex capped the needle. "So it's obvious that I'm tougher on the women than the men?"

"A little." Recruit Parker's smile was groggy. "But it's OK."

Alex closed the med kit. "I only do it because I know how much harder it is for women to be taken seriously in this field. If I don't prepare all of you"—she gestured to the other female recruits—"the world will eat you whole."

Recruit Parker blinked so slowly, Alex thought she might have fallen asleep. "OK" was all she said. And then she *was* asleep.

"Agent Danvers?" Recruit Espinoza walked over, not even giving a glance to her fallen classmate. "Can we run the maneuver again?"

Alex gestured to Recruit Parker. "After what just happened?"

Recruit Espinoza nodded. "We want to practice until we get it right."

Alex smiled but it was small and tight. She'd been waiting for weeks to hear that from her recruits, but after Recruit Parker's fall and manic drive to please Alex, she wasn't sure she wanted to witness just how far the recruits would go to make her happy.

Alex checked on Recruit Parker once more before getting to her feet. "Why do you want to make me proud?" she asked Recruit Espinoza. "Yesterday you called me Dictator Danvers."

Recruit Espinoza laughed. "That was yesterday! Today I think you're the greatest." The admiration in her eyes should've pleased Alex, but Recruit Espinoza had never struck her as a fickle person to change her mind so easily.

Alex frowned. She was getting exactly what she wanted from the recruits: respect, adoration, obedience, initiative.

So why didn't she feel like she'd earned any of it?

8

FAUST IS A DEAD MAN. FAUST IS A DEAD *man.*

Supergirl chanted in her head as she flew herself and Mon-El across town.

It was the only way to keep her mind preoccupied.

After zipping into costume outside Empire, she and Mon-El had headed straight for the DEO, Supergirl clutching Mon-El, and Mon-El clutching Kara's journalism bag (the last thing she needed was Lena thinking Kara lost the gown and glasses again).

A vivid imagination was great for an artist or writer, but not for a worried superhero who couldn't reach any of her DEO friends. Faust's illusions might not do physical harm, but the people he inflicted them on were another matter.

And who knew what he could be hypnotizing her friends to think? What if he had them all lined up on the roof of the DEO building, convinced they could fly?

Fortunately, a quick glimpse with her telescopic vision didn't show Supergirl any unusual activity around the DEO's building. *Un*fortunately, because the structure was lead-lined, she couldn't use her X-ray vision to see inside.

Supergirl was about to try her comms again when a bloom of orange light exploded from a building below. Citizens on the street screamed and scattered for cover.

Even though Supergirl was worried about the DEO team, she couldn't ignore the rest of her city.

"Hang on!" she shouted to Mon-El.

Supergirl tightened her grip on him and dove straight down, her stomach bobbing around in her chest. The orange light she'd seen came from the smoldering front doors of National City Bank and Trust, set ablaze by a hoodie-clad woman with fiery hands. For the briefest of moments, Supergirl thought Tlaca had finally gone overboard to help The Forgotten, but then she spotted a tangle of red hair peeking out from under the hood.

"Is that *Scorcher*?" Supergirl asked Mon-El, squinting.

Mon-El's arrival on Earth had coincided with an assassination attempt on the president. At first, Supergirl and the DEO had thought Mon-El was the culprit, but it had turned out to be an Infernian woman, nicknamed Scorcher. The funny thing was . . .

"I thought we had her in lockup at the DEO," said Mon-El.

"We did," said Supergirl.

Mon-El tapped her arm. "Wait a minute. Kara, isn't that Mandrax?" He pointed farther down the street, where a hulking, pointy-eared alien with a ridged scalp stood outside an auction house. Under one arm, he cradled a bronze statue.

Mandrax was an interstellar art thief and *another* criminal that should've been in the DEO's lockup.

"Faust let them out," Supergirl muttered. "He *must* have."

"Well, I hope they enjoyed their freedom," said Mon-El, securing the journalism bag across his body. "You want to take Scorcher while I take Mandrax?"

Supergirl smiled at him. "It's like you're reading my mind."

Supergirl changed course and flew past the auction house, releasing Mon-El, who latched on to Mandrax's back and wrapped an arm around the art thief's throat. Then Supergirl returned to the bank, zipping around Scorcher in tight circles to create an airless vacuum. Without oxygen, Scorcher's fire snuffed out, and she dropped to her knees, gasping for breath.

Supergirl landed beside her, and the vacuum dissipated.

"Trust me, you're going to prefer this to running out of air," she said, throwing a right hook that connected with Scorcher's temple.

The Infernian slumped against the building, unconscious, and Supergirl hoisted her over one shoulder.

A voice sounded in Supergirl's ear. "Supergirl?"

"Agent Vasquez!" Supergirl felt simultaneous joy and worry. "I've been trying to reach someone for ages! Where are Alex and J'onn? Are they OK?"

"They're . . . physically fine, ma'am. But—"

"They're hypnotized," Supergirl finished for her. She glanced down the street, where Mon-El and Mandrax were trading punches.

"Yes, ma'am." Surprise registered in Agent Vasquez's voice. "How did you know?"

"I did a little research on Faust," Supergirl replied. "Are Alex and J'onn the only ones incapacitated?"

"No, ma'am," said Agent Vasquez. "Everyone on the control room floor is . . . well . . . *on* the control room floor. Same for the floor below that."

"Where the prisoners are." Supergirl nodded. "That explains how they escaped. How many got out?"

Agent Vasquez sighed. "Seven, ma'am."

Supergirl almost lost her grip on Scorcher. "*Seven?*" She

leaped into the air, gazing up and down the street for more chaos. "What's the ETA on a strike team?"

Agent Vasquez was silent for a moment. "There isn't one, ma'am. When the prisoners started escaping, the strike team rallied to stop them. Now they're all hypnotized, as well."

Supergirl let out a guttural groan. "You've got to be kidding. Who's left?"

"Me, the recruits, and Pam from HR. Faust must not have made it down to our floor."

Supergirl closed her eyes. "Crap."

"Ma'am, with Director Henshaw and Agent Danvers incapacitated, you're next in command," Agent Vasquez reminded her. "What do you want us to do?"

Supergirl shifted Scorcher's weight on her shoulder and ran her free hand through her hair. She didn't have the answer to Agent Vasquez's question.

All this time, Supergirl had thought she was the best person to stop Faust, since she had the most magic experience. She'd thought everyone should defer to *her*, since her knowledge on the subject matter outweighed the others' on her team.

The problem was, knowledge alone wasn't enough.

Supergirl wasn't a tech wiz who could track down the other escapees and find Faust's magic; Winn was. She wasn't the commanding presence and reassuring father figure when things got tough; J'onn was. She wasn't a combat expert who could assemble a strike team and attack plan in ten seconds flat; Alex was. And she wasn't the manifestation of all that was human and moral; James was.

Supergirl couldn't defeat Faust alone. To beat him—to beat *all* her adversaries—she needed her team.

And they needed her, too . . . especially now.

"Ma'am?" Agent Vasquez prompted.

"Give me just a second," said Supergirl.

"Standing by."

Supergirl zipped over to Mon-El, who had Mandrax over *his* shoulder, wrists bound with rebar, and was opening the door to the auction house.

"We're returning this Broccolini sculpture." Mon-El held the statue just out of Mandrax's reach. "And you're going to apologize."

"*Boccioni.*" Mandrax grunted in pain. "The artist's name is Boccioni, you ignorant pretty boy."

Mon-El frowned. "Well, that was uncalled-for." He glanced back at Supergirl as she rummaged through the journalism bag. "Everything OK?"

"Not yet, but soon." Supergirl fished out the glasses Lena had given her. Tlaca's business card was wedged in one of the earpiece hinges. "Go ahead and take Mandrax inside to drop off the . . . Broccolini."

"Boccioni!" Mandrax hollered as Mon-El strode away with him.

Supergirl extracted the business card from the glasses and pressed the comms button in her ear. "Agent Vasquez? Call this number and tell Tlaca that . . . that Supergirl needs her help."

It pained her to reach out to the princess, especially given the negative things Tlaca had said about her, but she was out of options. And saving the city was much more important than saving her pride.

"Brief Tlaca on the situation and the escaped inmates. And tell her I'll owe her one." Supergirl read off Tlaca's phone number and ended the communication as Mon-El reemerged from the building with Mandrax.

"Here, I'll take him." Supergirl lifted Mandrax by one arm and slung him across her other shoulder as effortlessly as if he were a dish towel. "Can you round up the rest of the inmates?" she asked Mon-El. "Hopefully, Tlaca will be joining you, but I have to get to the DEO."

Mon-El nodded and started to answer, but Mandrax shouted over him.

"Lava! The ground is lava!" He pointed at their feet.

Mon-El and Supergirl looked down at the bubbling red liquid engulfing their boots. Then they looked up at each other.

"Faust," they said in unison.

Other people weren't as familiar with the illusion-ist's work. Up and down the sidewalk, people screamed and clambered on top of parked cars. A man barreled past Supergirl to get into the auction house, causing her to drop Tlaca's business card and Lena's glasses.

"Hey! The lava's not real!" she shouted after him.

"Whoa," Mon-El said from where he was crouched on the ground. He'd bent to pick up the card and glasses, the latter of which he now held up. "Do you see this?"

Supergirl glanced at the glasses. Or rather, through them . . . at the ordinary, lava-free sidewalk below.

"What—?" She took the glasses from Mon-El and put them on.

People were still cowering on top of cars, but there wasn't a drop of lava in sight.

She whipped off the glasses, and the lava reappeared. "These things can break through Faust's illusions!"

Mon-El grinned and rubbed his hands together. "What are we waiting for? Let's go find him. He's got to be some-where nearby for this illusion to work, right?"

Supergirl shook her head. "We can't risk getting hypnotized."

"What if *they* can break through that, too?" Mon-El nodded at the glasses.

Supergirl bit her lip thoughtfully. The DEO was only a couple of blocks away. It wouldn't take long to test his theory.

"I'll go find out," she told him, taking her journalism bag. "Watch for Tlaca and the inmates, and make sure these people don't kill each other." She gestured at the panicked pedestrians.

Supergirl soared into the sky with Scorcher and Mandrax, flitting two streets over to the DEO building. She landed on the balcony and almost stumbled down the steps at the sight of Alex, Winn, James, and J'onn all sitting on the floor, staring blankly ahead.

"Supergirl! Thank God you're here." Agent Vasquez dashed over with a group of anxious-looking recruits. Upon seeing Supergirl in the sapphire glasses, she balked. "And . . . um . . . cool frames."

"They'll be even cooler if they can do what I hope they can," she said, lowering Scorcher and Mandrax to the floor. "Take these two back to their cells."

Supergirl knelt beside Alex, stroking her sister's hair. "Alex? It's Kara. Can you hear me?"

Alex's only reactions were to blink and breathe.

Supergirl sighed and removed the glasses. "I hope this works," she muttered, securing them gently on her sister's face.

Alex continued to stare into the distance.

Then her eyebrows furrowed.

Her eyes shifted from side to side, as if she were taking in her surroundings. And suddenly she jumped to her feet, gasping, and swiped at her face, knocking free the glasses.

"Hey, hey, hey! You're all right." Supergirl wrapped her arms around her sister. "I've got you."

"Kara?" Alex's voice came out in a whimper.

"You were hypnotized by Faust," Supergirl said as Alex squeezed her tight. "Whatever you imagined . . . it isn't real."

Alex stepped back and nodded, exhaling deeply. "The recruits were practically killing themselves for me. Are they—" She turned and stopped at the sight of her hypnotized friends. "Oh my God." She ran over to Winn and waved a hand in front of his face. "Winn?"

"He's hypnotized, too," said Supergirl. "So's everyone on this floor and the one below it. The glasses you were wearing will snap them out of it." Supergirl bent to retrieve them. "They can break through Faust's illusions and . . . thankfully . . . his trances, too."

"And I knocked them off." Alex brought a hand to her forehead. "Are the glasses OK?"

Supergirl inspected the frames and lenses. "I think so. I wonder if Lena knew what they could do when she gave them to me."

Alex shook her head. "Lena's a woman of science, so that's doubtful. The two don't exactly mix." She held out a hand. "Let's get everyone back to normal and worry about where our luck came from later."

Supergirl passed the glasses to her sister, and Alex fitted Winn with them. His initial reaction was similar to Alex's, who was quick enough to remove the glasses before he flung them. After Supergirl and Alex assured him he was back in reality, Winn cheered and hugged them both.

Supergirl released him and gave Winn and Alex both a strange look. "What exactly did Faust have you guys hypnotized to believe?"

"That we were living in our ideal worlds," said Alex.

"Huh?" Supergirl cocked her head. "But you were both super freaked out."

Winn rubbed his neck. "Yeahhh. It turns out that as much as I know about Doctor Who, I don't know *anything* about scriptwriting for the show." He cleared his throat. "*My* ideal world."

Alex smirked at Winn. "Nerd."

"At least it's a step up from fanfic," Supergirl said with a grin.

Winn narrowed his eyes at both of them. "Let's just move it along, shall we?"

The trio approached James and bolstered him when he came out of hypnosis clutching his face.

"Dude, you're OK." Winn patted his back. "Faust tricked you."

"I . . . I can see!" James spun around. "And the DEO's still here!"

Alex raised an eyebrow. "Your ideal world made you blind *and* killed us all?"

James bent and breathed deeply, resting his hands on his knees. "Not all of you. Just Winn."

"Wait, what?" Winn stepped back.

"It wasn't real, Winn," Supergirl reminded him.

"And it definitely wasn't my ideal world," James added.

"It was Faust's plan for the Demons Three."

"Still . . . rude!" Winn huffed. "In *my* ideal world, you all got to ride in my private jet." He frowned at James. "*You've* just lost your seat, sir."

James straightened. "Fine by me. I'm just relieved none of it was real." He took another deep breath. "So, Faust hypnotized us and escaped, huh?"

Supergirl held up a finger. "Actually, he hypnotized you, freed seven inmates, and *then* escaped."

"What?" Alex turned to Supergirl. "You didn't mention that!"

"Mon-El and I already caught two of the escapees, and he's out there rounding the others up," she reassured her sister, ushering Alex toward J'onn's entranced form. "Free boss, yell later."

"Oh, man." Winn grimaced. "What do you think *his* ideal world was like?"

Supergirl thought back to when a Black Mercy parasite had trapped her in her thoughts, giving her the happy life she missed . . . with her Kryptonian family. "I'd bet anything his wife and kids are there."

Alex nodded. "He told me yesterday that on Mars, this would be Family Week. Let's try and pull him out as gently as possible."

Supergirl, Alex, Winn, and James sat in a circle around J'onn, Supergirl reaching out to hold his hand.

"Do it," she told Alex.

Alex leaned forward and gingerly placed the glasses on J'onn's nose.

J'onn's eyebrows twitched, his nostrils flared, and his eyes grew wet. He blinked and a single tear spilled over.

Supergirl's heart ached. They *had* pulled him from his ideal world.

"Hey, J'onn." She squeezed his hand and removed the glasses. "Welcome back. I'm sorry, and I know it's probably not as great as where you were, but . . . we need you."

The others nodded their assent, offering reassuring pats and soothing words.

J'onn brushed at his cheek and smiled at each of them. "You misunderstand my emotion. It's not sadness at leaving my thoughts. It's relief at entering reality."

"Was I dead in *your* ideal world, too?" Winn ventured, and James elbowed him.

"No one was dead." J'onn shook his head. "I was back with my wife and daughters, but the girls hadn't aged a day. Seeing them still as children, while deeply fulfilling, was also disturbing."

Alex rubbed his shoulder. "J'onn, I'm so sorry."

"Don't be," he told her with a kind smile. "I've lived with their loss for a long time. I know my wife and daughters wouldn't wish for me to be trapped with the ghosts of who they were. And neither would the rest of my family." He placed a hand over Alex's and squeezed Supergirl's fingers.

"No, we wouldn't," Supergirl said, going in a for a hug.

She felt another pair of arms join hers as Alex hugged J'onn, too. And then Winn. Even James gave J'onn a pat on the back.

J'onn sniffled and pulled away from the others. "So those glasses can break Faust's hypnotic spell," he said, returning to DEO director mode and examining the frames. "We should probably get to work freeing the other agents."

Winn cracked his knuckles. "And *I* should go find Faust. Luckily, we have that inmate tracker on him, so our puppy should be back at the pound in no time." He howled like a dog.

"But then what?" Supergirl asked. "Every time we've dealt with Faust, he's always been a step ahead."

"Agreed. We need to find the source of his power," said Alex.

"Or a way to block it," said J'onn.

"Why don't we start with the glasses?" James asked. "Maybe there are more pairs where that one came from."

"I'll ask Lena where she got them," said Supergirl, reaching into her bag for her phone.

"You do that. I'm going to take care of the other agents." J'onn held up the glasses. "Winn, we can't rely on these alone, so I'd like you to come up with an alternate way to block Faust's hypnosis."

"Thrilled to," Winn said, retreating to his computer. "I do *not* want to go back to my ideal world. Not while the BBC execs are still throwing tomatoes."

Alex leaned toward James. "Not that I want to retraumatize you, but . . . how did the DEO get destroyed in *your* ideal world?"

While Supergirl texted, she kept her ears open. She had to admit, she was curious, too.

James chuckled ruefully. "My ideal world was a crime-free National City, where all the bad guys were taken off the streets. I thought it was the best way to deal with the problem." He hung his head. "Unfortunately, people started to widen their view of what was a crime. Loitering in coffee shops and carrying anything that looked even remotely like a gun meant a prison sentence. National City became a police state."

Supergirl crinkled her nose. She couldn't imagine living in a place like that.

"The DEO tried to fight back and stand up for the little guy," James continued, "but the government shut it down and demolished the building." He scoffed. "Some ideal world, huh?"

Supergirl sent her text and lowered her phone. "You thought you knew what was best, James. Believe me, I get it," she said with a soft laugh. "I've been that person, too. But it doesn't work without input from the people who matter."

"The citizens of National City. Yeah." James rubbed his chin, gazing thoughtfully into the distance.

Supergirl nudged Alex. "What about you? Why were your recruits killing themselves?"

"*Almost* killing themselves," Alex corrected with an embarrassed smile. "Because in *my* ideal world"—she ducked her head and brushed her hair behind one ear— "they all . . . liked me."

"Aw." Supergirl wrapped an arm around her sister's shoulders. "You don't think they like you?"

Alex let out a sharp laugh. "I *know* they don't like me. They call me Dictator Danvers."

James broke out of his reverie. "Is that why you've been mean-mugging them?"

"Yes, but only because it's not a fair title!" Alex argued. "They think I'm hard on them, but I just want to help them."

Supergirl leaned back and crossed her arms. "You sound like Snapper. He's always telling me what to do, like I can't figure it out on my own."

Alex shrugged. "Yeah, well, maybe he's telling you because he's been there before." She poked Supergirl in the stomach.

Supergirl recalled Snapper's words: "*Don't you think I've learned a thing or two?*"

She sighed. "It doesn't work without input from the people who matter," she repeated her advice to James. "Like my boss."

"And my recruits," said Alex. She handed Supergirl her phone. "I think we need to have some conversations."

As the phone changed hands, it vibrated with a text from Lena.

"Oh, but not right now." Supergirl wiggled her phone. "Because we have some magical glasses to buy."

9

NIMUE'S PARLOR TRICKS.

Supergirl stared at the magenta curtains in the window and then back at the paper in her hand where she'd scrawled the name of the occult shop.

"Are you sure this is the right place?" Mon-El asked, peering through one of the dust-coated windows. "It doesn't look like it's been open in years."

"This is the address Lena gave me," Supergirl said.

"Do not be fooled by appearances," Tlaca added. "That has proven our downfall many times over."

Since Tlaca had come through for the DEO team and helped Mon-El recapture the inmates, they'd informed her of their plan to visit Nimue's. She'd insisted on joining to ensure the store owner wasn't a charlatan, but Supergirl had a feeling Tlaca was more interested in coming so she could stay in the loop.

Supergirl didn't mind; Tlaca had certainly earned the right.

"I still don't see why *I'm* here." Winn hugged his arms to his chest. "I'm an IT guy, not a ghostbuster."

Supergirl smirked but didn't comment, even though she longed to point out that Winn had been here once before of his own free will.

Winn and James had visited Nimue's when National City had been transformed into Ancient Rome, but because of the time reversal, neither remembered it. If Supergirl had learned one thing from her speedster friend Barry on Earth 1, it was that it was best for people not to know too much about how their lives were altered after a time shift.

"First of all, this is an occult shop, not a haunted house," Alex informed Winn. "Second, now that Faust is on the lam, we can't risk separating in case he impersonates one of us."

"That's right. We won't let him divide our ranks." J'onn made a fist with one hand. "Stronger together!"

"Uh-huh, OK. I'm going in last." Winn pushed James in front of him.

"What's the matter, man?" James asked with a smirk. "You scared?"

Winn narrowed his eyes. "I'm not scared. I'm danger-aware." He gave an overall body shudder. "Blergh! Déjà vu."

"Why don't *I* go in first?" Supergirl suggested, tugging on the door handle.

Bells jangled overhead to announce their arrival. Nobody greeted them when they stepped inside, but when the door closed behind them, Supergirl's ears popped, as if the air pressure had drastically changed. The room went silent, too, without so much as a grumble from the garbage truck driving past the store.

"It's quiet," Mon-El commented.

"Too quiet," Alex added.

"The way *all* feel-good movies start," Winn muttered, plucking an incense stick from a nearby display.

Supergirl used her X-ray vision to see through the shelves and spinning racks in the store. A sunken circle appeared in the center of the carpeted room, and on the circle's edge, a woman sat cross-legged. Supergirl curled her index finger at the others and wended her way toward the woman.

"Hello?" Supergirl ventured. "My name is—"

"Kara Zor-El." The woman's voice was a whisper on the wind. "I hoped you'd come. And you've brought allies. Good."

Supergirl skirted around a table of tarot cards, fanned out to display the artwork on the back. Mon-El picked up a few cards.

"Hey, Alex. Do you have any . . . flaming towers or swords through the heart?" he asked.

Alex swiped the cards from him and put them back on the table. "Not now."

"You're supposed to say, 'Go fish'!" Mon-El informed her as they kept walking.

Supergirl shushed him as they stepped down into the sunken circle. A raven-haired woman in a flowy magenta gown fluttered her eyelids, opening them to reveal irises of the same reddish-purple.

"Hello," the woman said, taking in Supergirl and her companions. "What interesting company you keep."

The others looked at one another, trying to figure out whom she meant.

"Thank you." Mon-El finally spoke up.

"You're welcome, Mon-El of Daxam," the woman said. "Always quick with a comeback, though time will never be on your side."

Mon-El swallowed audibly. "What a creepy thing for a fortune-teller to say."

"She's a seer, if I'm not mistaken," J'onn corrected, turning to the woman. "Which means you can access the past, present, *and* future."

"Right you are, J'onn J'onzz," the woman whispered. "But you should not let your past dictate *your* future."

J'onn shook his head. "I don't intend to."

A smile tugged at the corner of the woman's mouth. "Good."

Supergirl waved her arms. "OK, you clearly know us, but we don't know you. Are you Nimue?" she asked the woman.

"Among other names," Nimue said. "Your friend Barry Allen calls me Madame Xanadu."

Supergirl's eyes widened. "You know Barry?" She sat on the edge of the circle near Nimue. "You've been to Earth 1?"

"I've been to all Earths," said Nimue. "And I *exist* on all Earths."

"You must have amazing cell phone coverage," said Winn.

Nimue turned her gaze on him. "You wear humor as armor, Winslow Schott Junior. Embrace what you fear."

Winn wrinkled his nose and tilted his head. "Nahhh. I'm not really in a hugging kind of mood." He smiled tightly and stepped behind Alex.

"You're fine," Alex assured him.

"Alexandra Danvers, ever the protector." Nimue sized her up. "Protect less; accept more."

Alex raised an eyebrow. "Thank you for *that* tip, but I'm pretty sure I didn't ask for a character analysis."

James leaned toward her. "That's not very accepting."

"Shut up," she muttered.

"James Olsen," said Nimue.

"Here we go," he said, opening his arms wide. "Let me guess: Stop trying to improve the city?"

Nimue squinted at him. "You can't stop what you haven't started."

James chuckled, his hands landing on his hips. "Excuse me?"

Supergirl rested a hand on his arm. "Can we please focus?" She clasped her hands together and smiled hopefully at Nimue. "Any cryptic words of wisdom for me?"

"Yes." Nimue leaned toward her. "It will rain."

Supergirl's smile dropped and she wrinkled her forehead. "O-K. I'll carry an umbrella," she said. "Thanks."

"But you haven't sought me out for your futures." Nimue changed position and recrossed her legs. "You've sought me out for National City's."

"Exactly." Supergirl reached into her boot cuff and pulled out the sapphire glasses, offering them to Nimue. "These came from your store."

Nimue regarded the glasses but didn't take them. "I trust they served you well. Great lengths were taken to make sure they found you."

"They've been *very* useful," J'onn interjected. "We were hoping you might have more."

Nimue shook her head. "I'm afraid they're one of a kind. Thanagarian Nth metal is hard to find now that your enemies have claimed it."

Alex scoffed. "We have a lot of enemies. You'll have to be specific."

"She means Cadmus," Supergirl said with a sigh. She turned to Mon-El. "Remember those Nth metal cages they trapped us in when they wanted my powers?"

"Yep. I got shot in the leg." He shook his head. "That was not a fun day."

Tlaca's mouth was slightly ajar as she regarded the glasses with wonder-filled eyes. "Those are Nth metal? Magic-negating, gravity-repelling Nth metal?"

"The very same," Nimue said solemnly. "The frames are what dispel Faust's illusions and trances."

"*And* they repel gravity?" Mon-El reached for the glasses, and Supergirl passed them along. "Does that mean you can fly with this stuff? I've always wanted to fly."

"Good," said Nimue. She turned her attention back to Supergirl. "I am sorry to not have better news. Ask me your other questions."

Supergirl smirked. "You knew I had some, huh? OK, how can we block Faust's magic without Nth metal?" She lowered her voice. "And do you know where the Bell of Ulthool is?"

Nimue pressed her fingertips together. "To block his magic, you must obtain the source of his power. Every *Homo magi* has one. Faust's is the *Necronomicon*."

Tlaca gasped. "The book of blackest magic?"

Winn wagged a finger at Tlaca. "OK, see, even without the gasp and the terrifying description, I knew it was going to be bad. Nothing that starts with the Latin word for 'death' ends well."

"Where can we find this *Necronomicon*?" J'onn asked.

"Faust will need to keep it close," said Nimue. "He cannot cast without it."

"How close is close?" asked Alex. "In the same city? In the same room?"

"Within arm's reach," said Nimue.

Supergirl thought for a moment. She never recalled seeing a book in Faust's hand, but she did remember seeing Faust's hand in his jacket . . . a lot.

"Alex, remember when you asked if Faust had any tells, and I mentioned—"

"That he'd put his hand in his jacket?" Alex snapped her fingers and pointed at Supergirl. "*That's* where he's keeping the *Necronomicon*." She frowned. "Except we took his possessions when we locked him up, and the book wasn't on him."

Nimue shook her head. "You misunderstand. The book will not be on his person. It will be in his pocket universe."

A squeaking sound came from the vicinity of Winn, and Supergirl looked over to see both his clenched fists pressed against his cheeks.

"Are you serious right now?" he asked. "Pocket universes are . . . are a real thing?"

Alex raised a hand. "What's a pocket universe?"

"Only just the greatest thing ever!" Winn jumped to his feet. "Man, Faust is *worlds* smarter than I gave him credit for."

"Winn?" Alex stared at him. "That in no way answered my question."

Winn nodded and started pacing. "Right, sorry. We all know that there are multiple universes, right? That's how it's possible to have an Earth 1, Earth 2, Earth 3, and so on. BUT not all universes are made the same. Some might be larger and some might be smaller."

"Like the size of a pocket?" James asked.

Winn waggled his hand from side to side. "Eh . . . possibly. 'Pocket' is just a reference term."

Supergirl looked to Tlaca. "Can Faust do that? Access a pocket universe? I thought all he could manage was illusions."

"He has sacrificed a part of himself for immortality," Nimue answered for Tlaca. "And a part of himself to cast illusions. It's possible, then, he could also sacrifice himself to access a pocket universe."

Supergirl leaned forward, elbows on her knees, and studied the floor. "So, Faust is storing his *Necronomicon* in the pocket universe, and to use his magic, he needs to bring the book out." She shrugged at her friends. "We just need to give him a reason to use magic. Then we steal the book and destroy it."

"Yeah, but we can't destroy the book before we know where he hid the Wheel of Nyorlath and the Jar of Calythos," said Alex. "And he's never going to tell us."

"We don't need him to tell us." Supergirl looked at her sister. "He'll bring out the artifacts *and* the *Necronomicon* when he summons the Demons Three."

Supergirl's words were met with stunned silence from the rest of the group.

"Am I trapped in my nightmare world again?" Winn finally broke the silence, looking around at the others. "Because that sounds like a Nightmare World plan." He patted the area above his upper lip. "Except I don't have my mustache."

Mon-El frowned. "Wait a minute. Faust needs the Bell of Ulthool before he can summon the demons. We still don't have that."

Supergirl turned to Nimue. "Do *you* know where the bell is?"

Nimue regarded her for a moment before giving a slight nod.

"OK. I must dissent." Tlaca got to her feet and made an X with her hands. "We are not giving Faust the Bell of Ulthool."

Supergirl stood and faced Tlaca, holding up a cell phone. She pressed the speed dial for Agent Vasquez and shifted the phone to speaker mode.

"Vasquez here," the voice blared through the speaker.

"Agent Vasquez, have there been any more incidents of break-ins or burglaries since Faust escaped?" Supergirl asked.

"Yes, ma'am," said Agent Vasquez. "Several more *dragon-related* break-ins."

"Thank you, Agent Vasquez." Supergirl ended the call and spoke to Tlaca. "We both know Faust won't give up until he finds the Bell of Ulthool. And that means he'll continue to terrorize the citizens of this city, which I cannot allow."

"Yes, but if he unleashes the Demons Three, he can terrorize the world, which *I* cannot allow." Tlaca jabbed herself with an index finger.

"I won't let it get to that point," Supergirl promised. "I'll stop him as soon as he takes the *Necronomicon* from the pocket universe."

Tlaca crossed her arms and narrowed her eyes at Supergirl. "And why should I trust you? Your poor decisions have led us to this point."

Alex stepped toward Tlaca. "Hey—"

Supergirl held up a hand to silence her sister.

"I'll admit some of my choices haven't yielded the best results," said Supergirl, "but I made those decisions based on the knowledge I had at the time. And yes, there might be fallout, but I'm dealing with it."

"And are you prepared to deal with demons roaming the earth?" Tlaca challenged.

"Yes, we are," Alex replied before Supergirl could. "Because *I* choose to stand beside Supergirl."

She took her place next to Supergirl, who smiled as, one by one, J'onn, Mon-El, James, and Winn joined her.

Supergirl extended a hand to Tlaca. "Will you help us?"

Tlaca's nostrils flared and she pressed her lips into a thin line. "No. I will not be a part of this disaster. I am going to find Jason to clean up your inevitable mess." She spun on her heel and stormed toward the store entrance.

Supergirl let her arm fall and watched Tlaca leave, sighing. "Well, *that* sucks. Personality differences aside, she was a good ally."

"She will still be," said Nimue. "But not in this fight."

Supergirl smiled hopefully at the seer. "So, can you tell us where the Bell of Ulthool is, please?"

Nimue rose from the floor and studied Supergirl. "If I do, the burden of its protection shifts to you, Supergirl."

"No, it shifts to all of us," said J'onn, gesturing to the DEO team. "This is a group effort."

"We won't let Faust release the demons," Mon-El promised.

"Very well." Nimue glided on slippered feet to the front of the store. From the folds of her gown, she pulled a cell phone and held it up to the front door. With the press of a button, a woman's voice, youthful and exuberant, issued from the phone.

"Laever eht lleb!" the woman's voice said.

The jingling bells above the shop door shimmered and shifted, and a thimble-sized green bell appeared in their midst. Nimue plucked the bell like a fruit and handed it to Supergirl.

"You've had it *here* the whole time?" Supergirl marveled, cupping the bell in her palm. "How come Faust never picked up on it?"

Nimue smiled. "He isn't the only one with magical connections. I had help from a friend." Nimue pocketed her phone. "And now, Kara Zor-El, the last artifact is in your hands. You must find Faust, take back the artifacts he has stolen, and strip him of his power."

"She makes it sound so easy," Winn told James.

"Actually," Supergirl said, drumming her fingertips against her chin, "I think it *will* be easy. But we aren't going after Faust. We're going to make him come to *us*."

She craned her neck to glance back at her friends. "James? You spend a lot of time behind a camera. How would you like to be in front of one?"

James inclined his head. "What are you thinking?"

"We head to CatCo Plaza and broadcast a message, inviting Faust out to play."

Winn raised a hand. "Uh . . . I love playtime as much as the next guy, but won't that attract a lot of attention from curious citizens?"

"Not if we phrase it properly," said Supergirl. "Trust me, I'm a journalist." She winked. "We're good with words."

"OK, so James will send a hidden invitation to Faust. What do the rest of us do?" asked Alex.

"*You* two will head back to the DEO and ready a strike team." Supergirl pointed at her sister and J'onn. "And Winn, I want you to work with Maggie at NCPD to find a place we can meet with Faust without any civilian casualties."

"You got it," he said with a salute. "Callin' my girl Mags right now."

"Mon-El, you'll stick with James and me and help run defense in case Faust comes after James," Supergirl continued.

"It sounds like you've got a solid plan forming," said

J'onn. "But what happens once Faust meets us at this secure location?"

Supergirl rubbed her hands together. "We beat him at his own game."

10

THESE WERE ALL THINGS JAMES WOULD rather do than sit in his office at CatCo with a makeup artist hovering around him:

1. Listen to Winn rank his favorite companions on Doctor Who.

2. Stand in a two-hour line for broccoli.

3. Get kicked in the groin.

"Ms. Shilling, I have dark skin and *no* hair," he reminded the artist. "What could you possibly need to fix?"

"*This* for starters." She poked his cheek, and James flinched, remembering the bruise he'd gotten at the concert hall fight. "You're the current face of CatCo, Mr. Olsen. We can't have anyone questioning your character." She dabbed something from a bottle onto a sponge and then dabbed the sponge on his face. "Men always think they're too macho for makeup, but since our high-def cameras pick up every flaw, you're gonna thank me."

James eyed the bottle. "Just make sure it isn't obvious."

"Trust me," she said, blending the makeup into his skin. "I'm a master of disguise."

"James, I don't know why you're getting so upset over foundation," Mon-El said, sitting on the couch beside him. "On Daxam, they had an entire line of makeup for men."

Ms. Shilling glanced at Mon-El, and James flashed him a warning look. As far as anyone at CatCo knew, Mon-El was Mike Matthews, an average human who used to work in the office.

"Daxam?" Ms. Shilling repeated.

Mon-El formed an O with his mouth before smiling widely. "Yes! That's the name of a show I was on. A sci-fi drama." Mon-El nodded. "I played a captain. Captain Kirk."

James cleared his throat loudly. "Uh, Mike? Why don't you go look for Kara?"

"I'm right here." She entered James's office and smiled at the makeup artist. "Aw, Gerri, you're losing your touch! James still looks grumpy."

"Makeup can only do so much," Ms. Shilling replied with a sigh.

"You're both *very* funny," James said with a dry smile. "Are we all set, Kara?"

She nodded, touching a finger to the sapphire glasses she was wearing. "Everything looks great."

While James had been prepping for his TV appearance and Mon-El had been standing guard, Kara had scouted the building, wearing the Nth metal glasses to check for illusions.

Ms. Shilling stepped away from James and studied her work. "And *you* are ready for your close-up, Mr. Olsen."

"Just one more thing." Mon-El grabbed a powder puff from Ms. Shilling's kit. Before James could stop him, Mon-El patted it against James's forehead.

"'Ey! Get off me!" James pushed him away, and Mon-El tossed the powder puff to Ms. Shilling.

"That shine was driving me *crazy*," Mon-El said. "You're welcome."

Ms. Shilling left the office and James settled himself behind his desk, clipping a microphone to his lapel while the cameraman set up his equipment. Kara and Mon-El approached James, and Kara surreptitiously slid the Bell of Ulthool out of her purse and placed it front and center on his desk. To unwitting viewers, it would not even be noticeable, but Faust was sure to spot it right away. *If* he caught the broadcast.

"Are you sure Faust is going to see this message?" James now asked Kara in a quiet voice.

"When he and I first met, he told me he never misses *Lunchtime with Laurie*," she said, toying with a stapler on James's desk while she whispered. "Before the show starts, we'll air this, and Faust will see it. Trust me."

"All right," James agreed. "Let's do it then." He organized the notes on his desk and cleared his throat while Kara and Mon-El stepped out of the camera's view.

"Ready, Mr. Olsen?" the cameraman asked.

James nodded and awaited the countdown cue before smiling at the camera. "Good morning, National City! We know you're excited for *Lunchtime with Laurie*, but before we get to that, I wanted to share a new feature we're introducing in *CatCo* magazine. Something *you* can be a part of."

The idea had come to James after his horrifying vision of a dystopic crime-free National City and his conversation with Alex and Kara. The police, Guardian, and the DEO were working to stop crime, but someone needed to make an effort to keep it from happening in the first place. That meant encouraging citizens to make the right choices, and for *that*, they needed input from the people who mattered: each other.

James folded his hands on his desk. "There's been a lot of focus in the news lately on what's going wrong in the world, but nobody talks about what's going right. We at CatCo thought it might be nice to recognize the citizens of our city who are making it a better place for those around them . . . bringing hope for a better tomorrow and inspiring others to do the same."

Now came the tricky part.

"The idea for this feature came to us from CatCo viewer Felix Faust," James continued, keeping his expression as relaxed as possible. "Felix Faust, if you're watching, we've got a special gift for you. Call the number on your screen"— James spread his arms wide in front of him, making sure to center the Bell of Ulthool between them—"and we'll tell you where to claim your gift. To our other viewers, send an e-mail to the address on your screen with *your* inspirational story, and you just might see it featured in *CatCo* magazine." James smiled broadly at the camera. "Thank you, and have a magical day."

The cameraman motioned for the end of the recording, and James relaxed in his chair.

"Perfect!" Kara clapped and turned to the cameraman. "You can add in the phone number and e-mail address in the next thirty minutes, right?"

He nodded. "Sure, but Mr. Olsen, are you sure you want to put your office number on the air?" The cameraman frowned at James.

"Definitely," said James. "I'd like to talk to Mr. Faust directly."

"Then I'll get this down to editing," said the cameraman, and he began packing up his gear.

When he left, James looked at Kara and Mon-El and rubbed his hands together. "Now we play the waiting game."

"Now *you two* play the waiting game," Kara corrected, pointing at him and Mon-El. "I've got to get this bell to Alex." It jingled as she tucked it into the side pocket of her bag. "Call me as soon as you hear from Faust." She squeezed James's arm and kissed Mon-El. "And if Snapper comes looking for me, tell him—"

"That you're running personal errands on company time?" Snapper leaned against the doorway of James's office, arms crossed.

Kara's eyes widened and she pasted on a smile before turning to face him. "Hey, Chief!"

"I gave Kara permission to step out." James spoke up.

"Yeah, well, I didn't." Snapper nodded to Kara. "How's your award-winning story coming?"

"Uh . . . great!" She flashed him a thumbs-up. "It's really coming along." Kara chuckled. "In fact, you should just hand me the Wheeler-Nicholson Award right now!"

Worst lie ever, James thought.

"What is it?" Snapper asked.

"Hm?" Kara pressed her lips together and tilted her head. "What's what, boss?"

Snapper sighed and rubbed the bridge of his nose. "What's the award-winning story?"

James racked his brain for an idea to help Kara, but Mon-El interjected first.

"It's a surprise!" he declared with a triumphant smile.

OK, I was wrong, James mused. That *was the worst lie ever.*

Snapper didn't even grace Mon-El with a glare. "Ponytail—"

"Aw, man. You're calling me that again?" Kara asked with a pained expression.

"Why does it feel like I'm taking more of an interest in your future than you are?" Snapper finished.

"You're not!" Kara argued. "I care about winning this award, too. I just . . . I don't know *what's* going to win it." She settled on the arm of the couch. "You said I had to inform, educate, and entertain, but it's hard to find a story that does all three."

"You did it with both the alien fight club and supercitizen stories," Snapper reminded her.

James raised his eyebrows. Snapper might have been one of the few section leaders James constantly butted heads with, but the man knew talent when he saw it. Getting

Snapper to verbally acknowledge it was a challenge, how-ever, so his argument to Kara was almost high praise.

Kara seemed to know it, too. She smiled and shrugged. "I was in the right place at the right time," she said.

Snapper rolled his eyes. "*That's* a load of bunk."

"Bunk?" James crossed his arms. "Why do you say that?"

"I'd tell you, but it would involve me giving advice," said Snapper. "And our esteemed award finalist here"—he jerked a thumb in Kara's direction—"thinks she's above that."

Kara blushed and shook her head. "No, Boss, I'm not. I'm sorry I didn't let you help me before." She breathed deeply and clasped her hands in her lap. "If you have advice to give, I want to hear it."

It was the closest to speechless that James had ever seen Snapper.

Snapper nodded slowly. "All right." He leaned against the doorframe. "There's no such thing as right place, right time, when it comes to a story, Danvers. Good journalists take advantage of *every* place and *every* time, and great jour-nalists can make a story out of anything."

Kara held up a finger. "OK, I'm not saying I know better than you, but I *did* that with Princess Tlaca."

"You *started* a story," Snapper corrected. "You provided a list of facts, but then what? Where's the conflict? Where's the resolution?"

"I thought reporters were only supposed to give facts," spoke up Mon-El.

Snapper glanced over and scowled. "And you are?"

Mon-El raised his eyebrows. "I am . . . sorry I said anything."

Snapper turned his attention back to Kara. "If you want to talk about this princess and her charity, that's fine, but you need more. A nice lady who fund-raises for the underprivileged is how the story starts. What happens next?"

Kara nodded. "Got it."

"Good. Because I want the rest of the story by tomorrow." Snapper stabbed his index finger into his palm.

Kara hunched her shoulders. "Yes, Chief."

"And you two." Snapper looked from James to Mon-El. "Olsen and Aging Boy Band Member, quit enabling her." He turned and stomped off to scold someone else.

"Aging boy band member?" Mon-El furrowed his brow and then shrugged. "Eh, I've been called worse."

"OK, must add 'give Tlaca's mission a dramatic twist' to my list of near-impossible feats," Kara said, pressing a hand to her forehead. "And now I *really* have to leave."

"You've got this, babe!" Mon-El called as she rushed out the door. He turned to James. "Well, we have some time to kill. Want to help me work on a screenplay for *Daxam*?" Mon-El picked up a pen and notepad and settled on the couch. "Now that I've said it out loud, it sounds like a really good idea. Oh, and dibs on the role of captain."

James sat beside Mon-El and watched as he happily wrote the title across the top of the page.

"Hey." James nudged him. "I'm sure Kara's ideal world would have her working alongside Christiane Amanpour, and I know everyone else's. But what would *your* ideal world have been like?"

Mon-El tapped his pen against his lip and gazed out the window. Then he returned to his writing. "Nah, I can't tell you."

"What . . . come on, man. It can't possibly be *that* embarrassing," James coaxed.

Mon-El started a doodle of himself wearing what James could only assume was meant to be a captain's hat. "In my ideal world, I'd win an award, OK?" Mon-El asked, without looking up. "ForMostImprovedSuperhero." He said the words in a rush that took James a moment to comprehend. When he did, James smiled.

"That's great! Why wouldn't you want to tell me?"

Mon-El lowered his pen. "Because I don't deserve an award like that."

"What?" James wrinkled his forehead. "Why not? You've done a lot for this city."

"Yeah, but that's because of Kara." Mon-El gestured

toward the doorway she'd recently vacated. "If she hadn't encouraged me to be a better person, I wouldn't have gone down that path."

James smirked. "I think a lot of people could say that." At the confused look from Mon-El, he added, "Haven't you ever heard a famous person accept an award? 'I wouldn't be here without . . .' fill in the blank: a parent, a teacher, a coach. People can give you advice, but it's your choice whether you take it. And that choice is what gets you where you are. And the choice after that and the choice after that." James dotted the air with his fingertip.

Mon-El was quiet for a moment but sat a little taller. "True."

"So, when you finally win that . . . Most Improved Superhero award"—James snickered and so did Mon-El— "you can thank Kara and anyone else who helped you, but you should know that ultimately, it was your choice to take that advice that made the difference."

Mon-El grinned. "Yeah, maybe you're right." He extended a hand, which James clasped. "Thanks, man. You make me feel like I almost *could* captain a starship."

"I don't know . . ." James leaned back and crossed his arms. "I feel like Winn would fight you for the job."

"Please," Mon-El scoffed. "He's the engineer working the transporter, all the way."

James laughed. "OK, so you're planning to just rip off *Star Trek*?"

Mon-El frowned. "Star what?"

James raised an eyebrow and walked back to his desk. "Maybe you should see what else is out there before you start that screenplay." He flipped open a laptop.

Thirty minutes later, James and Mon-El had gone from staring at James's laptop to staring at James's desk phone. The message to Faust had finally aired, and even though they were expecting the call, when James's phone rang, he and Mon-El both jumped.

"This is it! This is it!" Mon-El rubbed his hands against his thighs in anticipation.

"Shhh!" James closed his office door and placed the call on speaker. "This is James Olsen."

"Hello, James Olsen, aka the Guardian," Faust replied in a teasing voice.

"It's just Guardian," James corrected. "Not *the* Guardian. I'm a hero, not a newspaper."

"A hero?" Faust laughed. "So says you. But I didn't call to discuss your delusions of grandeur. I called because, unless my eyes deceived me, you have something that I want, sitting on your desk."

"You mean the Bell of Ulthool?" James glanced past his

phone. "It *was* sitting on my desk. Supergirl has it now. You'll have to meet her in Magnus Park on the edge of town."

"Awww. The cute little place with the carousel horses and princess castle?" Faust clucked his tongue. "Bless her heart, she's still the sweet little girl from Midvale."

James shared a look with Mon-El. Faust knew an unsettling amount about Kara.

"Well, listen," Faust said, "I'd love to stay and chat, but I've got to get across town during lunchtime traffic, and you know what a pain *that* can be. Tell Supergirl I'll be there shortly!"

The call disconnected, and James flipped open his signal watch. "Kara, Faust is heading across town for the park."

"Copy that," she said. "I'm on my way."

"Us, too," James said, grabbing the bag that held his Guardian costume.

He might be far from keeping the city crime-free, but for now, he could at least keep it demon-free.

11

RECRUITS! WE NEED TO TALK!" ALEX
barked at her reflection. She made a face, softened
her expression, and tried again. "Team, let's chat.
You know . . . ugh." Alex cleared her throat and grinned,
throwing backward peace signs. "Whazzup—"

"Agent Danvers?"

Alex's hands snapped down by her sides, and she whirled
around. Recruit Parker stood in the doorway of the DEO's
debriefing room with a crowd of recruits behind her.

"Are you ready for us?" Recruit Parker blinked at Alex.
"Or did you need to finish your conversation?"

Alex tucked her hair behind ears that burned with
embarrassment. "No, no, I'm good. Please, come in." She
beckoned to the recruits.

Recruit Parker and her classmates filed into the room. Thankfully, Alex noticed, Recruit Parker carried her weight on *both* legs, her fractured tibia a gruesome consequence only in Alex's illusion.

It was finally time for Alex to do what she'd been dreading: acknowledge what the recruits thought about her, give *her* feedback, and find a compromise that worked for everyone. Her ideal world had everyone doing what she wanted, but that wasn't a way to live. It was a way to . . . well . . . dictate.

"Everyone take a seat, please." Alex gestured to the chairs she'd arranged. "We need to talk about something a little disturbing." Several recruits stared at the floor, no doubt ready for another upbraiding by Dictator Danvers.

Alex took a deep breath. "What's disturbing is my treatment of all of you."

The recruits said nothing, but their raised eyebrows and open mouths spoke volumes.

"As some of you noted, I've been a bit hard on you . . . especially the women. I want you all to succeed. I *really* do." Alex twisted her hands together. "But I'm also scared for you."

Alex felt her throat tighten a bit, so she stared at the lights overhead. "This country is working hard to bridge the gender gap, but in some fields, like this one, it's still a man's world. And to be a woman in a man's world means extra challenges." Alex pointed at the female recruits. "I want you to be prepared for those challenges."

Recruit Espinoza raised her hand. "Challenges like what?"

"Like . . . being pushed harder than your male counterparts in the hopes you'll give up," said Alex. "Or being criticized more because people don't think you belong."

"Director Henshaw would *never* do that to us," said one of the other female agents. Her teammates nodded and so did Alex.

"You're right. Director Henshaw is nothing but fair, and that's why I continue to work with him," Alex said. "But you might not stay at this job forever. You might choose a different department." She held open her arms. "And that's where the challenges come in. I want you to be prepared for whatever's coming."

The recruits were quiet for a moment, and then Recruit Espinoza raised her hand again.

"So you've been terrorizing us out of *kindness*?" Her voice rose into a squeak, and the other recruits laughed. Alex allowed herself a small smile.

"When you put it like that, I guess it does sound a little ridiculous." Alex pinched her fingers together.

"Ma'am, that's nice of you to worry," said Recruit Parker,

"but when you go harder on us, doesn't *that* say we're not equal to men?"

Several recruits murmured in agreement.

"Yeah, and how do you know we can't meet those challenges on our own?" added Recruit Espinoza.

Alex stared at the floor. The recruits were right.

When Alex had started at the DEO, she wanted to be treated just like everyone else and go through the same training regimen. If anyone had done to her what she'd done to the recruits, she would've been just as upset.

"I hear you," Alex said. "And I'm sorry. I'll make more of an effort to keep things balanced."

Recruit Jessup stood and patted Alex on the back. "Your heart's in the right place, ma'am."

Alex eyed him. "Your hand's in the wrong place, Jessup."

He jerked his hand away and scrambled back to his seat. "Sorry, ma'am."

The female recruits laughed and clapped.

"That's all we want," said Recruit Parker. "For you to get after the guys as much as you get after us."

"But we can't put this all on you," admitted Recruit Espinoza. "We should have said something to your face and not behind your back. We're sorry, too."

More agreement from the recruits.

"Apology accepted." Alex clasped her hands behind

her back. "Now, why don't we start over? My name is Alex Danvers, and I'll be—"

A speaker overhead crackled, and Winn's voice echoed around the room. "Hey, Alex? Faust is headed for the rendezvous point. J'onn wants you to assemble a strike team."

The excited whispers of the recruits grew so loud Alex had to lift her chin and shout to the ceiling to be heard.

"Copy that, Winn! Can you have Agent Vasquez come to the debriefing room to take over with the recruits?"

"Will do."

Alex lowered her chin and glanced out at the recruits, who had quieted down, their faces crestfallen and their shoulders slouched. Clearly, they'd been hoping to go on a field mission.

Well, she thought, *they need to get real-world experience sometime.*

"Hey, Winn?" Alex called to the ceiling. "Cancel that. The recruits are coming with us on this one."

"Yes!" Recruit Parker high-fived Recruit Espinoza. The other recruits chattered and wriggled in their seats until Alex quieted them.

"For this mission, you'll be running a diversion *without* firearms," she told them. "Felix Faust is a master illusionist, and he can make you think your teammate is the enemy. I'd rather you not shoot each other before graduation."

The recruits laughed.

"He can also hypnotize people, but Agent Schott is working on a way to prevent that. The most important thing to remember is that Faust is nothing more than an illusionist," said Alex. "Which means nothing he creates can harm you."

She turned to a map of National City and pointed out where the recruits would be stationed. During that time, Supergirl and Alex would stall Faust while J'onn, who could pass through objects, stole Faust's *Necronomicon*. As Alex talked, she occasionally heard a titter of laughter from one of the recruits, but she couldn't blame them. It wasn't every day your boss directed you to "traverse the troll bridge and seek cover in the fairy bushes."

"NCPD has already cleared the park and cordoned off the entrances, so there shouldn't be any danger to civilians." Alex faced the recruits once more. "Any questions?"

The recruits didn't say a word, and Alex wondered if that was for fear she'd change her mind and not let them come on the mission. *But* she had promised to trust them more, so instead of pressing the issue, Alex clapped her hands and pointed to the door.

"Gear up and meet by the vans in five minutes!"

Chairs scraped against the floor as the recruits scrambled to be the first out the door and into their tactical gear. Alex followed them down the hall but veered off to the DEO garage. J'onn and Supergirl were loading a black case into one of the vans while Winn tinkered with a satellite antenna on the roof.

"What channels can this thing get?" Alex joked, looking up at the antenna.

Winn spoke from the corner of his mouth, like an old-time repair man. "What channels *can't* it get, sweetheart? You want HBO? You got it." He switched to his regular voice. "Seriously, though, the satellite picks up trace magic, so we know when Faust is coming *and* if he's about to cast an illusion."

"Clever." Alex poked her head into the van. "And the locks are in place?" She rapped her knuckles on the case J'onn and Supergirl had loaded, and the case made a slight jingling sound. Inside was the Bell of Ulthool, secured with two biometric locks that required J'onn's and Supergirl's fingerprints to open.

"Faust isn't getting the bell without us," Supergirl assured her.

"Is the strike team ready?" J'onn asked Alex.

"They're gearing up," she said. "I thought I'd take the recruits out for their first mission."

Supergirl's eyes widened. "Against Faust? Are you sure they're ready?"

"As ready as we are," Alex replied. "This is the Department

of Extra-Normal Operations. They're only ever going to face the unexpected."

J'onn nodded. "Too true. Grab them and let's get going."

"Wait! One last thing." Winn slid down the windshield of the van and grinned. "Heh. That was as cool as I thought it would be."

"Winn?" Alex prompted.

"Right." He reached into his pocket and pulled out an orange pharmacy bottle. "Typhoid vaccine. You and your recruits should each take one." He tossed the bottle to Alex.

Alex popped the cap off and studied the pills inside. "Typhoid vaccine? Why? We're only going to the park."

"Because your boy called his childhood therapist"—Winn pointed to himself—"and found a way to stop the hypnosis: Keep the dorsal anterior cingulate cortex running at max capacity." He nodded his head along to the words of his sentence, as if reciting from memory.

Alex squinted. "That's the part of the brain that processes stimuli, right? So you can react to things?"

Winn nodded. "Hypnosis slows down activity in the dACC, and typhoid vaccine increases it. Your brain will clock overtime, and Faust shouldn't be able to hypnotize you."

"Works for me." Alex swallowed her vaccine and trotted back toward the building just as her recruits came sprinting out, looking terrified and ecstatic. As she distributed the vaccine to each one, she eyed the recruits' equipment. To her satisfaction and relief, all of them passed inspection.

"Roll out!" She smacked a palm on the hood of the lead van, where J'onn was riding, and climbed into the next van, sitting beside Winn.

"Meet you guys there!" Supergirl told them, zipping out of the garage.

Alex turned in her seat to look back at the recruits traveling with her. "Since we've only gone over it once, I want to make sure you understand the plan once we get to the park." While they traveled the fifteen minutes across town, Alex listened to the recruits in her van, then, over walkie-talkie, the recruits in the other van. By the time they'd reached their destination, bypassed the police cordons, and parked next to James and Mon-El, even Winn could recite everyone's positions.

"Make me proud," Alex told the recruits, and they jumped out of the van and fanned out, heading for their respective posts.

"Man, this place is nuts." Mon-El pointed to an enlarged park map as Alex joined him and James. "Web World with a giant spider slide? Captain Kiddieland?" Mon-El looked closer. "Oh, cool! A pirate ship!"

"I thought the guy who built this place was a robotics genius," said James. He was carrying his Guardian helmet under one arm, already having donned the rest of his suit.

"Will Magnus is *the* robotics genius," corrected Winn, toting a tripod in one hand and his laptop in the other. "If machines ever rise up to kill us, we're gonna want to be besties with him."

"So why a low-tech park?" asked Mon-El.

"If you were surrounded by machines all day, wouldn't you want an escape from it?"

"I guess that explains the solar-powered carousel," said Alex.

Supergirl touched down near the group. "Faust is already here, and he's waiting for us at the princess castle." She pointed across a pond where swans and ducks bobbed without a care in the world.

Alex turned to Winn, who had opened his tripod and was propping up his laptop on it. "Systems check."

Winn's fingers flew across the keyboard. "Oh yeah. I'm picking up a ton of magic from our little friend."

Alex turned to Mon-El and James. "Care to go for a stroll?"

James donned his Guardian helmet. "We thought you'd never ask."

While Alex, Mon-El, and Guardian ventured forth on foot, J'onn transformed into Martian Manhunter and flew overhead with Supergirl, the case containing the bell dangling between them.

"Winn? How are we doing on magic?" Alex asked over comms as she, Mon-El, and Guardian crossed the drawbridge to the castle. She glanced around as if checking out the park, but her eyes fell on a recruit crouched behind a cluster of moored swan boats and another recruit who'd taken position under the drawbridge.

"Doesn't look like the levels have changed," said Winn. "But Alex? I'm running a comparison of what Faust's magic looked like when he attacked Guardian in Little Bohemia, and the blue sparkle action is a lot higher now."

"What does that mean?" Guardian asked.

"I don't know," Winn admitted. "Maybe he picked up a magic trinket from somewhere? Just be careful."

Mon-El pulled open one of the palace doors, and there, at the far end of the room, sat Faust . . . upon a throne.

"Why am I not surprised?" Alex mumbled.

As they approached, Faust shifted in his seat, regarding them with an imperious smirk. Alex couldn't help noticing new lines around his mouth and wrinkles in the corners of his eyes. She also spotted a slight tinge of gray hair around his temples.

Was Faust's mortality finally catching up with him?

"Well, well. If it isn't the Three Meh-sketeers," Faust greeted the trio with an oversized yawn.

"Aw. Your yawn says 'bored,' but your eyes say 'tired.'"

Alex ran a finger from her own eyes to her temples. "And did we skip our Just for Men hair coloring today?"

Faust glowered at Alex. "I happen to look very distinguished with salt-and-pepper hair." He turned his attention to Guardian. "Now, where's my bell?"

"Right here," said Supergirl as she and J'onn touched down behind Alex, Guardian, and Mon-El. The case they were carrying hit the floor with a thud and a jingle. "But you won't be getting the bell unless you agree to some terms."

Faust's eyes lit up at the sight of the case. "And what, pray tell, makes you think you can keep me from the bell?" He pressed the fingertips of both hands together. "Your team is the most gullible group of people I've met since the accusers at the Salem witch trials. You really think I can't steal it from you?"

"Hey, Alex?" Winn's voice sounded in her ear. "The magic level just spiked."

"Kara," Alex whispered to her sister. "We've got incoming."

Supergirl crossed her arms. "Distracting us with questions while you conjure some illusions?" she asked Faust, approaching his throne. "That's fine. Even if you managed to steal the box, it won't open without two handprints, one of which is mine."

Supergirl held a hand out to Alex, who pulled the sapphire glasses from her pants pocket and placed them in

Supergirl's palm. "And you can't fool me anymore," Supergirl said, putting on the glasses.

"Really? Glasses *and* a cape?" Faust wrinkled his nose. "Honey, no."

"Guys, you know how weather maps look pretty gruesome when a hurricane's coming?" Winn asked. "Well, you're in the eye of a magical storm."

Faust rose from his throne and, instantly, everyone else shifted to defensive stances.

"You people truly infuriate me," Faust said. "With all your high-tech gadgets and high-level intellects, you still don't bother with the simplest things . . . like research. If you had, you'd know how the Demons Three are summoned."

"We *do* know," said Alex. "You need the wheel, the jar, and the bell."

"Yes! But what do they do?" asked Faust. "How do they work?" He spread wide his fingers, and an image materialized in the air of a silver wheel, a red jar, and a green bell.

Faust twirled one index finger and the wheel began to spin. He snapped his fingers and the jar of incense ignited, releasing a thin whorl of smoke. Faust stroked his goatee. "Now what to do with that last one?" He strode on tiptoe toward Mon-El. "Any thoughts on what to do with a bell?"

Alex's gaze shifted to the case at the same time Mon-El said in a grim tone, "You ring it."

"Exactly!" said Faust with a double snap of his fingers.

Alex thought of how the case containing the bell had jingled when she'd rapped on it with her knuckles, how the case had jingled when J'onn and Supergirl had taken off . . . *and* how the case had jingled when they'd dropped it on the ground.

Faust didn't need to open the case to make the bell work. He just needed the case.

Supergirl seemed to have a similar realization, and she dove for the case at the same time Alex did.

Unfortunately, a third party was also interested, and it sported *ferocious* claws and fangs.

With a roar, it barreled into Alex and Supergirl, batting them aside like Ping-Pong balls as it sank massive incisors into the case and loped away with it. Guardian leaped for the case but it slipped through his fingers, and he flopped to the floor.

"Tell me that wasn't a saber-toothed tiger," Alex said breathlessly.

"It's got the Bell of Ulthool!" J'onn shouted, giving chase.

"Did you say saber-toothed tiger?" Winn squeaked in her ear. "*So* glad I'm hanging out with the carousel ponies."

Mon-El looked from the crushed floor runner where the case had been sitting toward the castle entrance where J'onn and the tiger had disappeared. "What kind of illusion was *that?*"

Supergirl sat up, too, the sapphire glasses askew. "That wasn't an illusion," she whispered. "I could see it even with the glasses on."

"Oh. Did I not mention?" Faust returned to his throne. "Earlier today, I sold my immortality for twenty minutes of real magic to be used as needed." He ran his fingers through his graying hair. "Expensive, but I'll get it back when I've summoned the Demons Three. Plus, the looks on your faces were priceless!" he added with a snicker.

Supergirl charged toward the throne, but the illusionist turned magician held up his hand, and a glimmering wall appeared between them. Alex hoped her sister knew better than to touch it.

"If I were you, I wouldn't worry about me," Faust said. "I'd worry about what's going on outside."

He pointed behind the DEO team, and they turned. Alex could hear what sounded like screams and shouts.

"What did you do, Faust?" Supergirl demanded.

"It's *exhausting* coming up with ways to torture people," he said, "so I thought I'd draw from the surroundings."

Alex put a hand on her sister's arm. "Don't let him out of your sight. We've got this."

"It's cute that you think so!" Faust called as Alex, Mon-El, and Guardian sprinted toward the palace entrance. The doors were already thrown open from the tiger's (and J'onn's) earlier exodus, but the trio paused in the doorway just the same.

Scabbard-wielding pirates chased some of the DEO recruits while other recruits struggled in the web of a twenty-foot spider and still more recruits climbed into trees to evade trolls with axes. In the distance, Winn wobbled on the roof of a DEO van that was surrounded by bucking carousel horses.

"Go away! I don't have any sugar cubes!" he shouted.

Next to Alex, Guardian sighed. "Where do you want to start?" he asked.

"You take the pirates, and Mon-El, you deal with the trolls." Alex grabbed one of the castle's flagpoles, snapping it in half over her leg and tossing aside the banner-bearing end. "I've got a craving for spider-on-a-stick."

12

EIGHTEEN MINUTES.

Supergirl had to wait only eighteen more minutes for Faust to lose his real magic. By then, hopefully, J'onn would have the bell back from the saber-toothed tiger and could zip through Faust's body to steal his *Necronomicon*.

She sized Faust up while he batted his eyelashes at her.

"What will Supergirl do next?" he asked, tapping his chin.

She wondered the same thing. It wouldn't do any good to bargain with Faust. He clearly had the upper hand. And she couldn't attack him, either. He'd put up his defensive shield or run away.

And that brought up another question. Why *hadn't* he

already run away? His magical minion had the case containing the bell, so wouldn't it make sense for Faust to follow and make sure the tiger escaped? The trickster was too smart not to consider something like that.

Which meant he knew something Supergirl didn't.

"Ooh. You're thinking a little too hard, sweetie." Faust tapped the space between his eyes. "Here comes the Crinkle Fairy!" he said in a singsong voice.

"What are you waiting for?" she asked him point-blank.

"Nothing in particular," Faust said with a shrug. "I'm just enjoying having real power and the chaos it creates."

"You create chaos well enough as an illusionist," Supergirl said. She took a tentative step toward him, and instantly the viscous wall of magic appeared.

"Ah ah ah," he said, wagging an index finger. "Look all you want, but no touching."

Supergirl crossed her arms. "You realize in less than eighteen minutes, there won't be a magic wall to keep me from wringing your neck."

"Such violence!" Faust feigned shock. "And *you* realize a lot can happen in eighteen minutes. For example, the tiger I created could meet up with an angry mammoth who happens to enjoy goring Green Martians with its tusks." Faust's gaze drifted up to the ceiling, and he snapped his fingers. "You know what? I think it just happened."

Supergirl kept her cool, but alarm bells went off inside her head.

She leaped into the air and sped out the palace entrance. If Faust had put J'onn in danger, there was no telling what he'd done to the rest of her friends. Using her telescopic vision and superhearing, Supergirl watched Alex let out a war cry as she plunged a wooden pole into a gigantic spider's eye. Deeper into the woods, Mon-El was flipping an ax in the air and smirking at a troll in front of him while several DEO recruits tied another troll to a tree.

In Captain Kiddieland, Guardian had climbed aboard the pirate ship and was leading a team of DEO recruits in a skirmish with some pirates. And in the parking lot, poor Winn was hugging the roof of a van, looking miserable while some carousel horses kicked it.

Supergirl swooped down and picked up her friend, wrapping an arm around his waist while he wrapped an arm around his laptop.

"Oh, thank God," Winn said, leaning his head on her shoulder. "You know all those kids who beg their parents for a pony? They're stupid."

Supergirl couldn't help smiling. "Where's J'onn?" she asked, hovering in the air with Winn.

He propped up his laptop in the crook of one arm and opened it. "Uh, looks like he's in the prehistoric pit." Winn pointed to the far corner of the park. "He's surrounded by magic, so I'm guessing he's still fighting the tiger."

"Among other things," Supergirl mumbled, looking for a safe place to put Winn. "How do you feel about hanging out at the food court?"

"Where the scariest things would be pizza slices and French fries? I skipped lunch, so that's perfect." Winn frowned at his screen. "Uh-oh. There's been another magic surge in Web World."

He and Supergirl looked to where Alex had been battling the massive spider. The spider lay on its back, legs curled in, pole jutting from one eye. Alex was now freeing some DEO recruits from webbing that entangled them.

Suddenly, the spider's legs twitched and it flipped onto its stomach.

"Zombie spider!" Winn shouted. "Alex, there's a zombie spider!"

Alex frowned and glanced skyward at the sound of Winn's voice, unaware of the elephant-sized spider rearing up behind her.

"Alex, look out!" Supergirl gripped Winn tightly and dove toward her sister, one fist outstretched.

Just as she reached Alex, a DEO recruit leaped onto the spider's back and lopped off its head with an ax. The spider collapsed, and both torso and head reverted to sculpted metal.

Alex gaped at the spider and then at her recruit.

"Espinoza. Thank you," Alex said breathlessly, extending a hand to the woman.

Recruit Espinoza clasped hands with Alex. "Hey, if you can't count on me to have your back, do I really deserve to keep this job?" she asked with a grin.

Winn stared at the beheaded sculpture. "So . . . I'm pretty sure that thing's worth a few grand. The DEO has insurance, right? Or Super Glue?"

"With all the collateral damage we do? Of course we have insurance," Alex assured him. She nodded at Supergirl. "I thought you were watching Faust."

Supergirl shook her head. "He's not going anywhere . . . for some reason."

"What do you mean?" Alex chewed her lip. "You think he's hiding something?"

Supergirl started to answer, but a realization struck her, and she clutched Alex's arm. "Yes! He *is* hiding something. Faust is going to summon the demons at the princess castle. He brought the other two artifacts with him, and he's hiding them there!"

"Of course!" Alex smacked herself on the forehead. "Why wait and risk us foiling his plans?"

Winn raised a finger. "But we *are* going to foil his plans, right?"

"Absolutely," Supergirl said. "What time is it?"

"Time?" Alex repeated.

"Faust said he could access real magic for twenty minutes," Supergirl reminded her. "And that was at 1:44. If he was going to perform the ritual at any time, it would be while he's protected with real magic."

Alex twisted her wrist so Supergirl could see the time. "We've got ten minutes."

"I'll help J'onn, but just in case the tiger gets away with the bell, I need you, Guardian, and Mon-El at the castle to stop the tiger from reaching Faust," Supergirl told her sister.

Alex nodded. "I'll gather the recruits."

"What should I do?" Winn asked.

"Faust can put up a wall of magic to block us out." Supergirl handed him the sapphire glasses. "But Nth metal repels magic, right?"

Winn stared at the frames. "You want me to turn the Nth metal into a high-efficiency satellite antenna so that instead of transmitting radio waves, it transmits magic-dispelling waves that are focused off the satellite dish's sub-reflector and then bounced off the reflector surface where they're diffused enough to shatter a magical barrier?" He paused for a breath.

Supergirl blinked. "Actually, I was thinking you could

shape the frames into a knife and cut through the magic, but sure." She pointed at Winn. "That . . . thing you said."

"Where are you going to get the right kind of satellite dish on short notice?" Alex asked Winn.

Winn rubbed his palms together. "You did say the DEO had insurance, right?" He pointed to the roof of the park's office.

Alex sighed. "Let's go borrow a satellite dish." She shooed Supergirl away. "Go help J'onn. I'll send Mon-El and Guardian to cover the drawbridge into the castle."

"Good luck," said Supergirl. She crouched and propelled herself forward as fast as she dared, curving and dodging around trees to reach the prehistoric pit. With her X-ray vision, she spotted J'onn grappling with the tiger while a mammoth squeezed J'onn's midsection with its trunk. J'onn might be able to turn himself intangible, but Supergirl knew if he did that, he'd have to relinquish his grasp on the case. He was willing to fight to the death for its security.

Now he wouldn't have to.

Supergirl blasted forward, both arms extended, tackling the saber-toothed tiger around the middle. To her surprise, the case, Martian Manhunter, *and* the mammoth went tumbling across the pit with them, a cloud of dirt exploding as they landed.

"J'onn!" Supergirl released the tiger and reached for the

Martian. She couldn't help but be impressed that J'onn still clung tight to the case. To her annoyance, however, so did the tiger.

J'onn opened and closed his mouth, but no sound came out, the mammoth's trunk constricting his breathing. Supergirl blew a handful of dirt in the mammoth's trunk, and it recoiled, trumpeting and snuffling in an effort to clear its nostrils.

"I'm all right," J'onn assured her with a wheezing breath. "The tiger's teeth are caught in the case, though. Even if he wanted to let go, he couldn't."

Supergirl's eyes traveled from the tiger's teeth to the biometric locks on the case. "OK, so we let him have the case," she said, pressing her hand on the scanner. It beeped in confirmation, and one of the latches unclasped.

"Good idea," said J'onn, placing his hand on the scanner. There was another beep, and the second latch unclasped, the lid of the case popping open.

Supergirl reached inside and grabbed the Bell of Ulthool before snapping the case shut again. "Got it!" she said.

J'onn released the tiger, which sprinted away with the case in its teeth. "What do we do now?" he asked, leaning against a tree. "Faust will figure out we have the bell."

"Now we go back to our original plan," said Supergirl, tucking the bell into her left boot cuff, the right already occupied by another handy trinket. "Charm and disarm." Supergirl tugged at J'onn's sleeve and hovered above the ground until he joined her.

She couldn't help taking a little pleasure in the peeved expression on Faust's face when she and J'onn arrived at the castle. The saber-toothed tiger sat on one side of Faust's throne, the gnawed, empty case open beside it. On the other side of the throne, a circle similar in size to the tiger had been drawn on the floor, the Wheel of Nyorlath and Jar of Calythos resting inside a pentagram embellished at each point with a burning red candle.

"You think you're so clever, don't you?" Faust asked Supergirl as she continued to float in the sky. "Having my pet retrieve the case with nothing in it."

"We only took back what was ours," Supergirl informed him. "Now, do you want to negotiate for the Bell of Ulthool or not?"

Faust rolled his eyes. "Fine. What do I have to do?"

"I'll give you the bell if you agree to leave this Earth once you've summoned your demons," Supergirl said. "You have to take them to Earth 43."

Faust stroked his goatee. "The benevolent Supergirl is OK sending me and my demons to wreak havoc on another Earth?"

"I popped in and checked out who lives there," she said.

"They can handle you." Supergirl turned to J'onn and made a face. "*Lots* of vampires."

"Vampires?" Faust hopped up from his throne. "I am one hundred percent intrigued! You have yourself a deal. Put the bell on the floor and step back."

Supergirl and J'onn settled to the ground, and Supergirl did as instructed.

Faust stepped forward to grab the Bell of Ulthool, but as he walked, he snapped his fingers. With a rustling like sails gathering wind, the castle tapestries wrapped themselves around J'onn and Supergirl, yanking them back against the wall. Supergirl had the wind knocked out of her, but J'onn's head struck a sconce, and his eyes slid shut.

"J'onn!" Supergirl blasted her tapestry bindings with heat vision, freeing herself and then flying to him. "Why did you do that?" she demanded of Faust.

"In case you were planning to jump me," Faust explained, dropping his magical barrier long enough to pick up the Bell of Ulthool. He shook it with his thumb and index finger.

Ting-a-ling!

"Has a nice ring to it, doesn't it?" he asked.

Supergirl finally severed J'onn's tapestries and lowered him to the ground, checking his pulse. Satisfied that he was merely unconscious, she turned her attention to Faust, who stooped to align the bell with the other artifacts.

Faust pulled a palm-sized book from his inner pocket and began to chant.

The *Necronomicon*.

Supergirl's heart hammered in her chest.

She couldn't reach Faust.

She couldn't stop Faust.

And she'd lost her last bargaining chip.

Her only hope was that her friends might come through, which—

Supergirl's ears perked up as she heard thundering in the distance, and she smiled.

Which they always did.

Faust, too, heard the thundering, which grew louder and stronger, strong enough to shake the floor and tip one of his ritual candles, extinguishing it. "Oh, what *now*?" He tucked his book into his jacket and crouched to relight the candle.

Supergirl flew to the castle doors and gazed out at the road leading to the castle. Her hand went to her mouth and she stifled a laugh.

Winn, Alex, Guardian, and Mon-El leaned low over galloping carousel horses, a satellite dish towed behind them on a section of chain-link fence.

"Well, well, if it isn't the Four Horsemen of the Faustpocalypse," Supergirl said.

"Four horse*people*," Alex corrected with a grin. "And you don't have this situation locked down already?"

"Mistakes were made," Supergirl admitted with a sheepish look. "Winn!" She turned to her formerly horse-phobic friend. "There are no words."

"Right? *Right?*" Winn grinned, gesturing to the horses. "I fed them some electrical wire and it turns out they're super friendly!" He dismounted and patted his steed's neck. "I named this guy Copper. And hers is"—he pointed to Alex, and she raised an eyebrow. Winn cleared his throat. "*That's* not important now. Mon-El?"

"Yep." Mon-El leaped from his horse, winked at Supergirl, and hoisted the satellite on one shoulder. "Where are we setting up shop?"

Winn pointed to the castle entrance. "Here should be fine. And turn the dish toward His Majesty." He nodded at Faust, who was storming over, pushing his magical barrier forward with every step.

"*What* is going on?" Faust demanded.

"Oh, sorry." Supergirl scratched her head. "Did you *not* want satellite in the castle?"

"I want peace and quiet!" Faust roared.

Alex clucked her tongue. "I dunno. The way you're screaming seems to convey the opposite."

"Back up," said Guardian, stepping to the edge of Faust's barrier. "We've got work to do."

"Right!" Winn pulled out his laptop and connected it to the satellite dish.

"What is this?" Faust stumbled backward, brows furrowed. "What are you doing?"

Winn curled his lip and punched a button on his laptop. "Say hello to my little friend!" he said, gesturing to the satellite.

To Faust's credit, he knew something was amiss and sprinted back toward his throne, scooping up the artifacts. The satellite dish emitted a high-pitched whine, and the magic barrier he'd created crackled and shattered into a million pieces, fine as dust. The saber-toothed tiger next to his throne reverted to a carved marble statue.

Supergirl charged forward, grabbing Faust by the front of his jacket and lifting him into the air. She wrenched the artifacts from his grasp—but to her surprise, a quick X-ray scan of his jacket revealed no *Necronomicon*.

"Faust, it's over," she told him, letting go of his jacket to pass the artifacts to Alex. "Your magic's going to be gone in a few minutes. Just turn yourself in."

Faust's previously collected persona dissolved. In its stead appeared a wild-eyed, grinning lunatic. He reached into his jacket, and for a moment Supergirl hoped for the *Necronomicon*.

But Faust revealed a knife.

"I can always perform another sacrifice and make more magic," he said with a cackle. "And I've put trackers on those artifacts, so even if you take them, I'll find them. And you."

Supergirl marveled at the man in front of her. He was willing to sacrifice everything for power, and he wouldn't stop until he got what he was after. Faust was clearly desperate to be more than an illusionist, even if he was one of the best.

One *of the best*, she repeated to herself. *There were others.*

"I can see why you're not happy being an illusionist," Supergirl said after a beat. "I mean, Houdini eventually gave it up, and he was a master at it."

Faust threw back his head and cackled even harder. "Houdini? He was amateur hour."

Supergirl crossed her arms. "Then how come everyone's heard of him, but nobody's heard of you?"

Faust's insane smile shifted to a smoldering glare.

"Uh . . . Kara? Maybe you shouldn't anger the crazy guy with the knife," suggested Winn.

"Well, she's not wrong," chimed in Alex. Supergirl was grateful for the assist, even though Alex probably had no idea where her sister was going with the verbal jabs. "Houdini was brilliant. Faust . . . puts on little plays with people."

"Plus, Houdini made elephants disappear," added Guardian. "Faust can't do that."

"Elephant—*uh*!" Faust enunciated the last syllable. "One elephant! And it wasn't even real magic."

Supergirl snorted. "Neither is yours. If I had Houdini's skills, I could totally put your illusions to shame."

"Ooh." Mon-El rubbed his hands together. "Challenge extended!"

Faust narrowed his eyes. "Care to make a wager? I'd love to take those artifacts off your hands when I prove you wrong."

Supergirl smirked. "You won't, so, sure. And when I prove *you* wrong, you have to leave this Earth . . . without the artifacts."

"Challenge accepted!" Mon-El cheered.

Supergirl and Faust both looked at him.

"Sorry," he said.

"You'll have to turn off your little magic-dispelling device," Faust informed Supergirl.

"Winn?" she said without even looking back.

"Yep." Winn punched a few buttons on his laptop. The whine of the satellite stopped.

Faust reached into his jacket, no doubt pulling the *Necronomicon* from its pocket universe. Supergirl could've tackled him right then, but it wasn't worth the risk. Especially when she had a much subtler way to get the book.

"Houdini's skills you want," said Faust, "Houdini's

skills you shall have!" He snapped his fingers, and Supergirl cracked her knuckles.

"Come on, Kara! You got this!" Mon-El cheered.

"Show him who's got the talent!" Alex added.

Faust shrugged and smiled. "Well? Impress me."

"OK, but stand back." Supergirl pushed on Faust's chest and bodily moved him. "I'm going *big* with this." She threw her arms wide, smacking Guardian hard in the stomach.

"Oof!" He doubled over and Supergirl winced, turning to check on him.

"Sorry. You OK?"

"Great." He clutched a hand to his midsection as he stumbled away.

Supergirl giggled self-consciously and toyed with one of her boots. "He'll be fine." She cleared her throat and stood with her hands on her hips. Everyone leaned in with anticipation.

"You know what?" she said. "*I* should probably get farther back."

Her friends groaned.

"Kara! You have two minutes before the real magic wears off." Alex tapped her watch.

"I know, I know. But I've only got one shot at this." She backed away to where Guardian was still hunched over. "And—"

"Don't quote *Hamilton* at me," her sister warned.

"*Fine.*" Supergirl rubbed her palms together, closed her eyes, and then splayed both hands in front of her. The air inside the palace filled with fireworks of every color and type, from waterfalls to brocades to crossettes, ending with a large smiley face.

"Oooh! Aaah!"

Her friends all applauded and Faust joined in with a long, sarcastic clap.

"That's the best you can do?" he asked. "Something you can purchase from a roadside fireworks stand?" Faust sneered at Supergirl and snapped his fingers. "Watch *this*."

Nothing happened.

Supergirl raised her eyebrows. "I'm watching."

"Hang on." Faust glanced down and shook out his hands. "I must have—"

He flicked one of his wrists at Alex.

Still nothing.

"Did you turn that *thing* back on?" Faust pointed at the satellite.

"Nope," said Supergirl with a smug smile. "What happened? Did you misplace your magic?"

"Did I—" Faust reached into his jacket and froze. "No." He patted his pockets. "No!" He ripped off his jacket and shook it. "My book! Where is it?" he shrieked.

"Which book?" Supergirl looked over her shoulder at Guardian. "This book?"

Guardian straightened up and pulled his hand from his stomach, palm-side up.

There, nestled in his fingers, was the *Necronomicon*.

"Hey!" Winn pointed at the book as Guardian passed it to Supergirl. "You?" He turned to Supergirl. "How?"

Supergirl reached for her waistline and pulled out the trinket she'd shifted from her boot to her belt: the interdimensional extrapolator.

After her last visit to Earth 1, Cisco Ramon, Barry Allen's tech genius BFF, had given it to Supergirl so she could reach the S.T.A.R. Labs teams any time she needed to. She figured they probably wouldn't mind holding one measly book for her.

"For my next trick . . ." Supergirl pressed the extrapolator's center button, and an interdimensional window appeared.

"Stop!" Faust screeched, sprinting toward her.

"That's *my* line." Mon-El extended an arm and caught Faust by the throat, flipping him on his back.

"I've always wanted to make something disappear." Supergirl flung the *Necronomicon* through the interdimensional window to Earth 1.

"Nooo!" Faust scrambled toward the portal. Without his book, he was no more than a mere man, and all it took was Alex grabbing his arm and twisting it behind his back to stop him.

"Hey! Who's throwing creepy books through the space-time continuum?" A Hispanic man with long, dark hair appeared on the other side of the interdimensional window. When he saw Supergirl, his scowl shifted to a smile. "Oh, hey, Kara!" He glanced around and waved. "Whoa, it's the whole Super Circus!"

"Hey, Cisco," Supergirl said with a smile of her own. "Do you mind holding on to that book for us? *He* can't be allowed to have it." She pointed down at Faust, who was sobbing into the floor.

"Eesh." Cisco wrinkled his nose. "Your perpetrator wears a purple suit?" He snapped his fingers. "The Purpletrator!"

Supergirl and the others laughed. Faust moaned.

"We'll be happy to hold on to it," Cisco told Supergirl, lifting up the book. "*And* we'd love to see you if you ever need a vacay from fighting villains at . . ." He gazed at the castle behind her. "God, tell me that's not your version of Disneyland."

Supergirl chuckled. "It isn't, and thank you for your help. Tell everyone I said hi!"

She pressed the extrapolator button again, and the window disappeared. Faust let out another sob.

"How did you do it?" he asked. "How did you take my book? I always keep it close to my heart." He patted his chest.

Supergirl stood in front of Faust, hands on hips, while Alex cuffed him and dragged him to his feet. "You gave me Harry Houdini's skills, remember? He might not have been as good an illusionist as *you*." Supergirl straightened Faust's jacket and took his knife. "But I hear he was one heck of a pickpocket."

13

COPPER, SILVER, GOLDIE, AND DASH. Those were our horses' names," Winn told J'onn. The two of them, along with Supergirl, Alex, Mon-El, and James, were in the debriefing room the next morning, sharing their accounts of what J'onn had missed. Winn sighed wistfully. "Man, I wish we could've kept those noble steeds."

"*I* wish I could've seen you all ride up to the castle," J'onn said with a chuckle. "I expect it was quite a sight."

"It wasn't as impressive as Winn makes it sound," said Alex. "They were plastic carousel horses, and mine had gum behind its ear." She made a face. "I touched it twice."

"So then we ripped the satellite dish off the park's

office roof and pulled up a piece of fence to carry it on," Winn continued.

"We?" Mon-El raised his hand. "Uh . . . I believe *I* did those things." He glanced from Alex to J'onn. "Unless you're keeping track of collateral damage, in which case I was completely against the idea."

"Nice save, babe." Supergirl patted his shoulder.

"Regardless of the damage, I'm very impressed by the use of Nth metal as a signal transmitter," said J'onn. "Based on the visitor we've got in maximum security holding, I assume it was effective."

Even though Faust was now powerless, Supergirl and Alex had agreed that it might be best to keep him under surveillance for a while. Since he was as crafty as he was crazy, there was no telling if he had any more hidden talents up his sleeve, and they already knew he'd do anything to achieve his goals.

Supergirl nodded at J'onn's question. "We shattered his magic barrier and stole all his artifacts."

"How did you get hold of his *Necronomicon*?" asked J'onn.

"I tricked him," Supergirl said simply. "I had him unknowingly give me the ability to pick his pocket, and I stole the book."

That was something she wished J'onn had been awake

to see. From the moment Supergirl had pressed a hand to Faust's chest and lifted his book to the moment she'd swung her arms wide and passed the book to Guardian, the whole scene had been straight out of a heist movie.

"You're lucky I caught on to what you were doing," James commented.

"I knew you would," she replied with a smile. "I only make friends with smart people."

"Yeah, we *all* knew the entire time what was going on," said Winn, rubbing the back of his neck. "Nobody freaked out."

"Hey, you were in on the supercitizen plan a couple of months ago, and most of the rest of us weren't," Alex pointed out.

Supergirl took her sister's hand. "Thank you for trusting me." She looked around at her friends. "All of you."

"Where are the artifacts now?" J'onn asked.

"Locked away in a place only Supergirl and I know," Alex told him. "We're going to meet Tlaca and Jason Blood and hand them over."

J'onn nodded his approval. "And the *Necronomicon*?"

"It's out of this wooorld!" Mon-El said in a wavery, mystical voice. At a look of zero amusement from J'onn, he added, "Literally. Earth 1. With some friends of Kara's."

"Barry Allen," Supergirl supplied. "The *Necronomicon* will be safe there."

J'onn nodded again. "I trust Mr. Allen and his friends." He clapped his hands. "Well done, all of you! Alex, I'd like to have the recruits in here for debriefings of *their* experiences in the field."

"Of course," Alex said, getting to her feet.

Supergirl had thought it bold for Alex to bring the recruits on such a potentially dangerous mission, but she'd been humbled almost as much as her sister by how adept the recruits were. She'd feared for their safety, but only two recruits ended up in the infirmary for minor injuries while the others had made it out with bruises, scratches, and amazing stories.

After Alex gathered the recruits and brought them to J'onn, she joined Supergirl to retrieve the artifacts for transport.

"You know, when all is said and done, I'd call that one of our more successful missions," Alex said as she and Supergirl both placed their hands on biometric scanners.

"Really? After everything we destroyed in the process?" Supergirl asked with a smirk.

J'onn was definitely going to have a difficult conversation with Will Magnus about the destruction of his park.

"I said 'successful,'" Alex repeated. "Not cheap. But

yeah. I'm glad I talked things out with the recruits and let them run a mission. Especially since one of them saved my life."

The scanners on the door flashed green, and Alex pushed it open.

Supergirl snorted. "Please. I totally would've saved you if she hadn't."

Alex turned to Supergirl. "You got there right when I was about to be a spider snack."

"And I would've pushed you out of the way and taken your place," Supergirl said with hands on hips.

"Aww." Alex stroked Supergirl's hair. "You would've sacrificed your life for me?"

"What? No!" Supergirl scoffed. "I would've exploded out of the spider's stomach." She raised both fists in the air and gave her sister a teasing smile.

"Touching," Alex said.

They entered the secured room and loaded the artifacts into a case similar to the one J'onn and Supergirl had carried to the park.

"Are you sure we can trust this Jason Blood guy?" Alex asked as they walked back up the steps to the control room. "I looked him up and he's a demonologist, so he's got the same freaky interests as Faust."

"Except he *banishes* demons," Supergirl said. "We can trust him."

They were halfway to the balcony when James grabbed Supergirl's arm, a cell phone against his chest.

"Hey, I'm glad I caught you guys." He looked from Supergirl to Alex. "Are you free for brunch on Sunday?"

"Whaaat?" Supergirl drew back her chin. "James Olsen is setting up a brunch?"

"With an omelet station!" Winn shouted from his desk.

James grinned. "My mom is coming to town this weekend."

Supergirl pressed a hand to her heart. "Aww, I love your mom! I'll absolutely be there."

"Me, too," Alex said. "Can I bring Maggie?"

"The more, the merrier!" James held his arms open and pressed the phone to his ear. "Hey, Ma? They can come."

"He seems to be in a better mood," commented Alex as she and Supergirl climbed to the balcony.

"Yeah." Supergirl grinned. "I think he has hope he didn't have before."

"Created by you?" Alex poked her in the shoulder, and Supergirl shook her head.

"No, believe it or not, he did that all on his own." She held her arm out to her sister. "Ready?"

Alex gripped the case tightly in both hands and nodded. "Let's do this."

It took less than a minute to reach the roof of Plastino Plaza, where Tlaca and a man with white-streaked auburn hair were waiting.

"Jason Blood!" As soon as Supergirl and Alex touched down, she released her sister and approached him with arms open wide. "You know the drill."

"Oh, right," he said with a sigh. "You do this sort of thing." He smiled and hugged a chuckling Supergirl. "Always saving the day, aren't you?"

"Better than lighting things on fire," she told him, stepping back with a smirk.

Alex pointed to Supergirl and then Jason, narrowing her eyes. "I know all my sister's friends, but not you. How do you know each other so well?"

"It's a long story," said Supergirl. "We go *way* back."

"Ancient history," added Jason.

Tlaca stepped forward and Supergirl felt herself stiffen for a scolding. To her surprise, however, Tlaca extended both hands and clasped one of Supergirl's in hers. "I am sorry I doubted you."

Supergirl relaxed and clasped her other hand over Tlaca's. "It's OK. I understand why you were worried. And you were right at times when I was wrong. I'm sorry I didn't listen more."

Tlaca smiled. "I suppose that is all water under the

bridge. Thank you for bringing the artifacts to us."

"Is this them?" Jason knelt beside the case.

"Yep." Alex eyed him as he flipped it over to show the biometric locks. "What do you plan to do with them?"

"Faust will not be the last person to seek them out," said Tlaca. "So, we have found protectors for each one *and* new homes."

Supergirl squatted beside Jason and pressed her hand on a bio scanner, unclasping the latch. "If you ever need help again, you can always call," she said.

Alex stooped and did the same thing, and the case sprang open. "Do you have a safe way to transport those?" She nodded to the artifacts. "We can reconfigure the bio locks for your handprints."

"That won't be necessary," said Jason, tucking the artifacts into his pockets. "Nobody would dare steal from us."

Supergirl smiled, knowing "us" wasn't himself and Tlaca, but himself and the demon Etrigan.

"We should go," Tlaca said. "I have one last city official to meet with who *was not* at the gala that I might persuade to help my charity."

The Forgotten, Supergirl thought to herself.

"The other city officials won't help your cause?" she asked.

"After they saw me attack the gala guests?" Tlaca asked

with a dry laugh. "I am lucky to still have *CatCo* magazine running a story on me."

Tlaca's story.

Supergirl had pushed it to the back of her mind while dealing with Faust. Now that *he* was taken care of, she had to come up with a better way to tell Tlaca's story, or the princess wouldn't get help from *anyone* in National City.

"Too bad there aren't a bunch of rich people around here who could use a little excitement," Supergirl said. "What you need are a bunch of bored, retired—" She paused and widened her eyes. "Tlaca, can you be at 27 Wayne Street in an hour? I know someone who might be able to help you."

"One hour? Do we have the time to spare?" Tlaca looked to Jason, who nodded.

"I can start the trip by myself," he told her. "You take care of your people."

"Great!" said Supergirl. "My friend will see you then." She reached up and hugged Jason, then held her arm open for Alex, who shook Tlaca's and Jason's hands before joining Supergirl.

"And this helpful friend of yours would be . . ." Alex said.

"Kara Danvers, of course," said Supergirl.

Alex nodded. "*Of* course. Say, you wouldn't mind

dropping me off in Little Bohemia, would you? I want to do some crystal shopping."

Supergirl regarded her sister with amusement. "Crystals? Are you going the Wiccan way?"

Alex shook her head and smiled. "More like the Martian way. J'onn may not be able to get his official Family Week on Mars, but I figured we could throw him an unofficial Family Day at James's brunch, complete with crystal crowns."

"Ooh! I like that plan," said Supergirl. "Little Bohemia, here we come!"

An hour later, Kara was pacing outside 27 Wayne Street, also known as Empire.

"Hello, Kara." Tlaca strolled toward her, smiling. "Or should I call you 'Supergirl'?"

Kara froze. "What?" Her hand traveled to her face to make sure she was wearing her usual glasses disguise. "What do you mean?"

Tlaca rested a hand on Kara's arm. "Nimue referred to Supergirl as Kara, Alex referred to Supergirl as her sister, and I know Alex's last name is Danvers, as is yours."

"Ah." Kara's cheeks warmed. "I will have to have a little chat with her."

"Your secret is safe with me," Tlaca assured Kara. "But knowing this makes me like Supergirl all the more."

Kara couldn't help smiling. "Really?"

Tlaca gestured at Empire's front door. "So what are we doing here?"

"Finding you some donors." Kara ushered Tlaca up the steps. "That is . . . if you're willing to let new people on your board of directors."

Tlaca chuckled. "If they have the funds, I can find them a seat at the table."

"Perfect!" Kara opened the door to the club and flashed Lena's platinum card. She hoped Jonathan Cheval would have no place better to be in the middle of the day, and she was relieved to find him sipping coffee in an armchair.

"Mr. Cheval?" Kara ventured.

"Miss Danvers!" he boomed. "Are you here for the rest of my story?"

"Actually, I wanted to introduce you to someone." Kara motioned Tlaca forward. "Do you remember Princess Tlaca from the museum gala?"

Mr. Cheval lowered his coffee mug and got to his feet. "Do I remember her? Of course! Quite a spitfire you were!" He offered Tlaca a hand. "Who was literally spitting fire," he said with a chuckle.

"Throwing it, actually," Tlaca said with a laugh of her own. "Only to protect what was mine."

"I like that!" he said, indicating an empty seat.

"Um . . . speaking of protecting what's hers," spoke up Kara, "Princess Tlaca runs an organization for indigenous peoples in her home country."

"Yes." Tlaca smiled at Mr. Cheval. "And while we are always looking for funding, we could also use board members with strong business acumen."

"Well!" Mr. Cheval puffed out his chest. "I have both in spades."

Kara watched and listened as Tlaca told Mr. Cheval about The Forgotten and then shared the story with other wealthy men and women who happened by, eager to lend advice *and* funding.

Then a realization struck her.

This was the missing piece of Tlaca's story!

The princess had seen others struggle and had fought to help them, only to struggle herself and now be helped by others. The best example of kindness rewarding kindness.

Kara pulled a notepad from her purse, scribbling frantically as conversation whirled around her.

Nimue was right; Tlaca had proven to be an ally, in more ways than one. Kara was glad that, despite their differences, they'd still managed to come together in the end to keep the world safe. And as Kara listened to the princess and the club members speak, she thought about how many other great things were accomplished with teamwork . . . how many great things the *DEO* had accomplished with teamwork.

As Kara Danvers or as Supergirl, her job was made profoundly easier by the people around her.

And when she won her first journalism award, whether it was the Wheeler-Nicholson or the Pulitzer, she'd be sure to thank them all.

ACKNOWLEDGMENTS

Always, always, always for family, friends, fans, and God

For Pam Bobowicz and her never-ending patience throughout this book

For Kara Sargent, who stepped up and brought this story home

For Jenn Laughran, who makes sure I get paid

For Ariel Rodriguez, my supportive husband and comic-savvy beta reader

For Sergeant Noel Guerin of the Austin Police Department, who helped me find Faust's "tell"

For Austin Books & Comics, who always have the resources I need

For the late Gardner Fox and the late Mike Sekowsky, who originated the Felix Faust story

For Elliot S. Maggin and the late Art Saaf, who created the original (and slightly more evil) Princess Tlaca

For the writers, cast, and crew of *Supergirl*, who inspire these stories through the characters they create.

ABOUT THE AUTHOR

JO WHITTEMORE is the author of numerous fantasy and humor novels for kids, including: The Silverskin Legacy trilogy; *Me & Mom vs. the World*; the Confidentially Yours hexalogy; and *Lights, Music, Code!*, a series novel for Girls Who Code.

Jo is a member of SCBWI (the Society of Children's Book Writers and Illustrators) and is part of the Texas Sweethearts and Scoundrels. She loves to make people laugh, and when she isn't tickling strangers, Jo writes from a secret lair in Austin, Texas, which she shares with her husband.

READ ON FOR A

SNEAK PEEK OF

THE FL

BY BARRY LYGA

ASH

THE TORNADO TWINS

My name is Barry Allen, and I'm the fastest man alive.

A particle accelerator explosion sent a bolt of lightning into my lab one night, shattering a shelf of containers and dousing me in electricity and chemicals. When I woke up from a coma nine months later, I found I was gifted with superspeed.

Since then, I've worked to keep Central City and its people safe from those with evil intent. With the help of my friends Caitlin and Cisco at S.T.A.R. Labs; my girlfriend, Iris; her brother, Wally; and my adoptive father, Joe, I've battled time travelers, mutated freaks, and metahumans of every stripe.

I've tried to reconcile my past, learned some tough lessons, and—most important of all—never, ever stopped moving forward.

I am . . . the Flash.

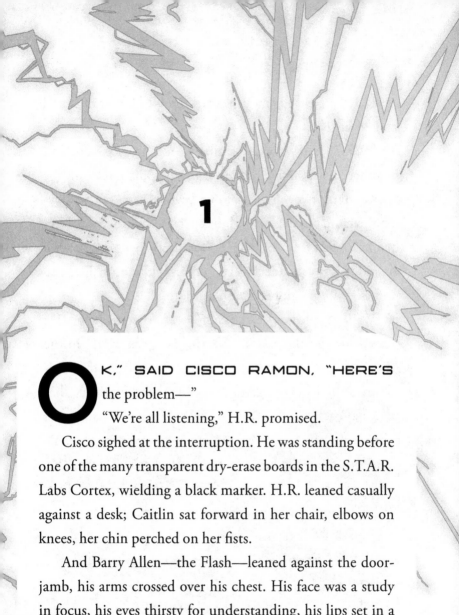

OK," SAID CISCO RAMON, "HERE'S the problem—"

"We're all listening," H.R. promised.

Cisco sighed at the interruption. He was standing before one of the many transparent dry-erase boards in the S.T.A.R. Labs Cortex, wielding a black marker. H.R. leaned casually against a desk; Caitlin sat forward in her chair, elbows on knees, her chin perched on her fists.

And Barry Allen—the Flash—leaned against the door-jamb, his arms crossed over his chest. His face was a study in focus, his eyes thirsty for understanding, his lips set in a grim, determined line.

"Go on, Cisco," he said calmly. "H.R., please be quiet."

H.R. opened his mouth, then thought better of it and saluted instead.

"We all know about parallel worlds," Cisco said, and he proceeded to draw a series of overlapping circles on the board. "Fifty-two variants of our own universe, all occupying the same physical space but separated by vibrational frequencies. So far, so easy." He paused, as though expecting an interruption, and glanced meaningfully at H.R., who mimed pulling a zipper over his mouth.

With a pleased expression, Cisco continued. He drew a line on the board. "So, this is one universe in the Multiverse. Time flows in one direction—from the present into the future. Again, easy. But there's a theory that says that each universe in the Multiverse contains its own specific variants. That each choice we make in *this* universe splits the timeline, creating alternate versions." He sketched scattered lines branching off from the main line. "Eat pizza for lunch—that's one version of the future. Eat a P, B, and J—that's another one. Most of the variants aren't different enough to matter. You'd never notice the difference—"

"Unless you looked at your napkin," H.R. offered.

Cisco groaned. "You'd *rarely* notice the difference. But in some cases . . . In some cases, there are big enough changes that one version of the future could be unrecognizable as compared to another. Same timeline, same universe, different outcomes."

The board was now a flurry of lines breaking off from the main one. It seemed hopeless.

"Lotta possibilities," Cisco continued. "We need to make sure you find your way through all this mess to the proper future, the *one timeline* that results in the Hocus Pocus who came back in time to challenge you."

More silence. You could almost hear brains churning.

"All water runs to the sea," Barry said into the quiet.

Everyone turned to him. "What was that?" Caitlin asked.

Barry strolled to the board and took a red marker from the cradle. "Pretend the main branch of the timeline is a river. All these breakouts that Cisco drew"—he circled a bunch of them in red—"are what potamologists—people who study rivers, H.R.—call distributaries, where the water flows outside the normal bed. But . . ."

At the mention of the word *distributaries,* Cisco flinched. Barry noticed but said nothing and went on. With a flourish, he began extending the distributaries, adding to them with his red marker, curving them back until they reconnected with the main timeline again, then circling big red loops around the terminus, where all lines intersected.

"For the most part, bodies of water flow from smaller to bigger to biggest. Distributaries eventually become tributaries, which recombine with the main river and flow to the biggest body of water, the sea. Or, in this case, the future."

Cisco shook his head. "Yeah, I've thought of that, but the more I brain it out, the more I'm not so sure we can apply water-table physics to time travel. It works as a metaphor, but does it actually *work*?"

"If you don't like earth sciences, how about simple algebra?" Barry challenged. "It's possible to have multiple, different factors that lead to the same answer. Say x-squared equals four, and you're trying to solve for x."

"Even I know this one!" H.R. chortled. "Two!"

Barry shook his head. "Nope. There are *two* answers: two and negative two. Square either one of them, and you get four."

Cisco was pacing and—quite unconsciously—vibrating just the tiniest bit. Only Barry, with his speed-attuned vision, noticed it. "I'm still not sure," Cisco mumbled. "Algebra and potamology can't match up to quantum weirdness and metaphysics.

"And then there's also the matter of speed," he went on. "The tachyon harness is busted but good, and it's gonna take a long time to fix it. Which means you've got no speed boost. You've broken the time barrier before, but in the *other* direction, going into the past. And even then, only by a day or so.

You're talking about traveling thousands of years and in the other direction. No offense, bro, but I'm not sure you've got the speed."

Barry grinned broadly. "Don't worry about speed. That's not an issue any longer."

Caitlin turned in her chair, raising an eyebrow. "Not that I don't appreciate the confidence, but would you like to share with the rest of the class?"

"Yeah, show us what you've got under the hood, B.A.!" H.R. crowed.

Barry ignored them and considered his friend for a moment. Cisco had always been a bit headstrong and usually concerned about safety. Not to this degree, though. His attitude was almost always, *Let's throw some science at this and do damage control later!* Now, he was being uncharacteristically cautious.

"Is there something I should know?" Barry asked gently.

Cisco cracked his knuckles and seemed suddenly too aware of Caitlin's and H.R.'s presence. He sidled up to Barry. "Can we talk? Alone?"

Barry arched an eyebrow. He liked to keep things out in the open. Fewer opportunities for hurt feelings and misunderstandings. But, sure. Cisco had earned a little privacy.

He threw an arm around his buddy's shoulders and guided him out into the hallway.

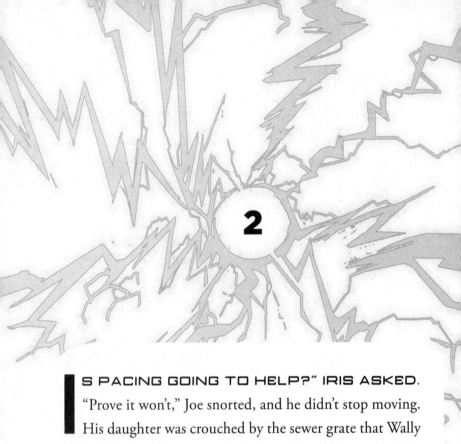

2

IS PACING GOING TO HELP?" IRIS ASKED.

"Prove it won't," Joe snorted, and he didn't stop moving. His daughter was crouched by the sewer grate that Wally had disappeared into hours before. She passed a smallish gadget back and forth over the opening. Something Cisco had whipped up.

"No chronometric deviations or quantum breaches," Iris reported.

"What about skid marks or broken mortar or—?"

"Cisco's device doesn't check for that sort of stuff. It's just telling us that Wally didn't get sucked into a breach or zapped into an alternate reality or ramrodded into the time stream."

"Yeah," Joe said, his voice laden with sarcasm and parental fear, "because those are the only dangerous things that could possibly—"

Just then, the street beneath them . . .

Vibrated.

Wally shut his eyes tightly. For some reason, it was less scary being trapped in the dark when you were making the darkness yourself. As a child, when he'd been afraid of the dark—the stillness, the occasional hacking cough from his mother dying in another room—he'd squeeze his eyes closed, and the dark became *purposeful*, not something to be feared. It worked again here and now.

Except for the rats.

They raced toward him in the filthy water, their bodies plashing and rippling. Any second now, they would be on him. Cisco's suit would provide some protection, but his face was unprotected, and it was too easy to imagine small, sharp teeth sinking into his flesh, stripping back his cheeks, laying bare his skull . . .

Settle down, West. That's not how a hero goes out. You've faced down some bad nastiness before, and you're not about to shuffle off this mortal coil as rodent chow. No way. No how.

He was still backed up against a wall. *No rats coming from that direction,* he thought. Could rats crawl down walls from above? *Ugh. Don't think about* that. *Focus on what's ahead.*

With both hands in the water, Wally braced himself against the floor and kicked his feet at superspeed. A roar filled the chamber as water thrummed and churned. Anything caught in its path would be knocked down, knocked over, knocked out.

With more and more fury, he kicked. The water rose and crashed, a mini tsunami there in the sewers. The floor and walls around him shook. Sediment filtered down from the ceiling, causing him to cough, but he kept up his speed.

Within moments, the rats had scattered. A few slick, furry bodies brushed past him, but they were harmless now, crushed and broken by the sheer force of the water he'd riled.

Water pressure. Not just a fact but a friend!

He grinned to himself. OK, so the rats were no longer a threat. And the silence in the chamber told him that Earthworm was gone.

Good.

He opened his eyes.

It was still pitch-black.

He was still trapped.

OK, but two out of three ain't bad . . .

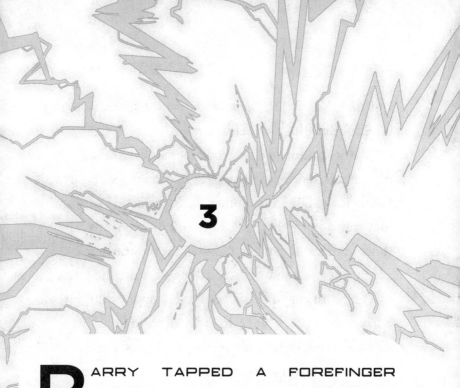

3

BARRY TAPPED A FOREFINGER against his chin as Cisco finished speaking, his voice excited and hushed at the same time. The story he'd just told Barry was both shocking and illuminating. And perhaps the most unexpected thing Barry had heard in the years since he'd gained his speed and become the Flash. He'd fought time travelers and madmen and a persnickety techno-magician. Just recently, he'd returned from a particularly thorny alternate universe.

And now Cisco was telling him . . .

"We're living in an alternate timeline?" Barry said.

Cisco shrugged. "Hey, look, personally, *I* think *they're* the ones living in the alternate timeline, with their Flashpoint and their Savitar and some dude named Julian. We're the original. But whatever. Semantics."

Barry remembered well the night after defeating Zoom, the night he'd decided to go back in time and stop Reverse-Flash from killing his mother. Iris's presence had stopped him from doing that, and he'd only infrequently cast his thoughts back to that possibility in the months since.

But now here was Cisco, telling him that he'd vibed a meeting with *another* Cisco, this one from a reality in which Barry had, in fact, gone back in time, stopped Reverse-Flash . . . and, instead of creating a personal paradise, he'd botched the job, making a reality that was so flawed that he had no choice but to go back in time *again*, this time to let his mother die and set things right.

Only, according to that other Cisco, things *hadn't* gone right. The reset hadn't put the universe back the way it had been originally. Some glitches came through from Flash-point: the villainous "god of speed" called Savitar, a set of dangerous powers and a split personality to boot for Caitlin.

Dante's death . . .

"You see why all this alternate timeline stuff is making me extra nervous, right?" Cisco said. "What if you run to the future but end up stuck in the Flashpoint future? Or something like that?"

"Cisco, I—"

Cisco grabbed Barry and pushed him against the wall. Panic and worry spun in his eyes. "What if you go and *we can't get you back?*"

Barry bristled at Cisco's physicality, but he realized it came from genuine anguish. Cisco wasn't being a bully; he was being a scared friend.

"It'll be OK," he told him. "We'll make it work."

Cisco stepped back, running his hands through his hair over and over again, telegraphing his anxiety. "How can you be so sure we'll figure it out?"

Barry grinned. "Because we always *do.*"

With a tight, humorless smile, Cisco shook his head. "I wish I shared your boundless confidence right about now, buddy. We're in uncharted territory here. If you were going a few days or even a few years into the future, I might not be so worried. Heck, if you wanted to jog a mere four hundred years to the twenty-fifth century and beat the snot out of Eobard Thawne when he was a punk kid, I'd probably sign off on that. But we're talking *millennia* into the future. Who knows what kind of quantum weirdness we'd be talking about? So many variables, and now we *know* that alternate timelines are a factor. You could end up in a different where, a different *when.* You could find yourself in a timeline where you're a different *you.*"

"Possibly," Barry mused aloud, "but do you know who I've been thinking about this whole time?"

"Rosario Dawson?" Cisco shrugged. "No? Just me? OK, who?"

"Georg Wilhelm Richmann."

"Who?"

"He was a Swedish scientist obsessed with Ben Franklin's experiments with electricity. He decided to duplicate the whole kite-and-string-and-key bit and got smacked in the head with a ball of lightning that ended up killing him."

Cisco nodded slowly. "I'm waiting—patiently, I might add—for the part where the story has a happy ending."

"My point is that this is what we do, Cisco." Barry clapped a firm hand onto Cisco's shoulder. "We risk. We charge in. We challenge the unknown. A couple of years ago, a ball of lightning smacked *me* in the head. Should have killed me. Guess what? Still standing. Sometimes you're Ben; sometimes you're Georg. What follows is what matters."

He beamed broadly at Cisco, who sighed in defeat. "Your endless, ennobling optimism is becoming really annoying. Let's figure out how to get you to the future, you pain in my butt."